Look for More Titles by Cassandra Chandler

Kral: A Scifi Alien Warriors Romance

Cygnian 7
Book Two

Cassandra Chandler

Copyright Page

This book is pure fiction. All characters, places, names, and events are products of the author's imagination or used solely in a fictitious manner. Any resemblance to any people, places, things, or events that have ever existed or will ever exist is entirely coincidental.

Kral: A Scifi Alien Warriors Romance
Cygnian 7, Book Two
Copyright © 2021 by Cassandra Chandler
Print ISBN: 978-1-945702-89-1
Digital ISBN: 978-1-945702-88-4

First eBook edition: October 2021
First print edition: October 2021
10 9 8 7 6 5 4 3 2

cassandra-chandler.com
P.O. Box 91
Mission, Kansas 66201

Chapter One

Family dinner night was not the time to be thinking of the maddening restlessness that was consuming Becca. Ever since Christmas, it had been growing in her—a strange sense of *something* that kept her awake at night. She thought it might have started with her brother, Buddy, announcing his first ever serious relationship to the family right around then.

Settling down had never been high on her agenda. Her family came first, and she hadn't met a guy she felt was good enough to be part of that.

She'd always thought that was something she and Buddy had in common. Seeing him settle down made her wonder if maybe it was time for her to consider it, too. The idea of a house and a picket fence and a regular nine-to-five set her teeth on edge, though. That life was not for her.

The restlessness chose that moment to rise up in her almost irresistibly. She paused on her way to the table, staring at the front door and imagining dropping everything and running outside. She wasn't sure where she'd be running to, though.

Or to who.

"Watch it," Amy said, ducking underneath the serving plate Becca had been carrying into the dining room from the kitchen.

Amy wasn't just the youngest sibling—she was also the smallest, even though she was in her early twenties. She still had to bend over to miss the plate that was heaped high with Mom and Buddy's spectacular cooking. Dad was pouring drinks as the middle sister, Sophie, put down the last of the utensils.

Shaken from…whatever that had been, Becca headed back to the table.

She wished they could do family dinner more than once a month. Then again, as she surveyed the epic feast on the table, she realized what a massive undertaking that would be. It was a miracle their big family could coordinate their schedules, especially now that Buddy was so busy with Nika.

He barely even had time to help out with running his own business. Becca had needed to take over much of the management of his sub shop while he was off helping his girlfriend.

What was he even doing to help her? Nika was some kind of high-end mechanic or engineer or something. Buddy was a chef—albeit an incredible one.

"Excuse me." The man himself swept into the room

with the main course, his apron stained from cooking.

Pickles and Dazzle, the family's two Pomeranians, danced around Buddy's ankles, their heads craned back to keep the dish in sight. They barked as if hoping they could startle a piece of meat into falling to the ground.

"Get," Becca said, waving the little orange fluffballs away. "Go to your beds. Can't you be more like Dash?"

Sophie's border collie looked up from her bed where she'd been lying in a civilized manner since Sophie instructed her to, a huge smile on her doggie face. Pickles let out a chuff, but both little dogs scurried away.

"Sophie, you're a professional dog trainer," Becca said. "You have to teach us what to do about these pom-poms."

Sophie shook her head. "I think they're beyond me."

Becca pushed some dishes aside to make room for the main dish. Roasted potatoes, carrots, parsnips, and onions surrounded the prime cut of meat. She took a deep breath, leaning over the dish and savoring the aromas.

"Buddy, this smells amazing," she said.

"Of course it does." He nodded, staring at the dish as if he was still looking for ways to improve it. He must not have found any, because he took off the oven mitts he'd been wearing and picked up the carving knives she'd laid out for him earlier.

The rest of the family hurried in, drawn by the scent, no doubt. Becca sat next to her mom, who had the place of honor at one end of the table, with her dad at the other end and Sophie and Amy across from her. Buddy sat at Becca's side.

The conversation between Becca's sisters and parents filled the room, along with the clatter of dishes. It was a nice distraction, but not enough to mask her agitation.

There was something she needed to do. Somewhere she needed to go. Something was…missing.

One leg bounced under the table and goosebumps rose along her arms. The goosebumps flowed up to her neck, then down her spine. She hadn't known she could even get goosebumps there.

"I can't believe Hayley is missing this," Amy said, pulling Becca's attention back to the table. "Couldn't she have come home from her trip a few days early?"

"She knows we'll fill our fridge with leftovers." Sophie passed her plate to Buddy to get loaded up and the rest of the family followed suit.

"Or, you could just come here to eat them," Mom said. "We'd love to see her. It seems she's always traveling lately. We've barely been able to visit since she came back from Paris."

"You and me both," Sophie murmured.

Hayley was Sophie's best friend and had practically grown up with her and Becca. She'd lost her parents way too early, and Sophie and Becca had moved into her parent's house with her as soon as Becca finished high school. They still lived together, over a decade later, though Hayley was often gone with her work as a travel writer.

Something had happened in Paris that neither Sophie nor Hayley was talking about. It was yet another thing driving Becca crazy. How could she help them if she didn't know what was going on?

"You're quiet today," Mom said.

Becca smiled. "I was just thinking that we need to do this more often. And next time Hayley really does have to be here."

"I absolutely agree." Mom reached over to squeeze her hand. "And Nika, too."

"She has important work, Mom," Buddy said, as he finally turned his attention to his own meal.

Becca bumped her shoulder against his. "Yeah. Maintaining the fleet of vehicles her billionaire boss owns is such important work."

Buddy had just picked up his fork and knife, but set them back down and turned to her. "Brendan Sloan is not her boss. And you have no idea how many lives her work impacts, so why don't you back off."

"Jeez, Buddy." Becca rolled her eyes. "I'm just saying, it seems like she should be able to get away every once in a while to spend time with your family. Especially since it's looking like we're going to be her family, too, someday."

Dad broke into the conversation. "All the more reason

for you to give her a break, Becca."

"I think what Becca is trying to say is that we'd all like to get to know her better," Mom said. "But we can be patient. And we can be civil at our own family dinner, since those also don't happen as often as we'd like." She cast a pointed look at Buddy and Becca.

"Sure thing, Mom," Becca said. He mumbled an agreement as well.

Sophie arched an eyebrow at Buddy and said, "Are you ever going to tell us how you landed such a classy woman as Nika?"

Buddy half-smiled as he lifted a bite of roast potato. "Through my cooking, of course."

Everyone laughed and some of the tension seemed to ease.

Honestly, Becca hadn't meant to set Buddy off. She was just trying to tease him. Maybe goad him into opening up a bit.

He'd been so wound up lately. And he wasn't confiding in her like he used to. He was keeping secrets, and she hated that she couldn't pry them out of him.

The conversation had just started again, although a little more subdued, when Buddy's watch started beeping. He set down his utensils and looked up at the ceiling.

"You gotta be kidding me," he mumbled. He somehow managed to swallow the bite he'd just taken and stood, backing away from the table. "I have to take this."

Becca swiveled around in her chair to watch him retreat. "Seriously? During family dinner?"

"I'll be quick," he yelled, already in the kitchen.

Mom reached over to squeeze Becca's hand again. "Come on, honey. Leave him be."

"Yeah, Becca," Sophie said. "Buddy's never had a girlfriend before. Give him time to work things out."

"If he keeps on like this, by the time he works things out, we'll *never* see him," Amy stated sharply. "I get that Nika is important to him, but he needs to remember that we're important, too."

"Let's hear it for baby sis." Becca raised her glass just as another wave of goosebumps rocketed across her body. This time, they *started* on her spine and radiated out to cover her back.

What the hell was going on? To make things even more confusing, tingling warmth spread through her stomach and pooled in her belly and…lower.

That was awkward.

The Pomeranians both leapt from their beds and ran to the foyer, yapping loudly. Even Dash sat up, her ears perked in their direction. Mom yelped as someone pounded on the door. Not knocked, *pounded*. Becca swore she felt the floor shake beneath her feet with each blow.

"What the…" Mom pressed a hand to her chest. "What is it now?"

"I'll get it." Sophie rose, gave Dash the signal to stay

put, then headed toward the living room.

It must be nice having a dog that listened.

"So much for a peaceful family dinner," Dad said.

Buddy hurried back from the kitchen. He didn't sit down. Instead, he grabbed Becca's arm and started pulling her out of her seat.

"We have to go," he said. "Now."

The urgency in his voice gave Becca a chill. She'd never seen such a serious expression on her big brother's face. Not even when he'd caught her making out with Brock Rhodes under the bleachers and dragged her back to their high school.

"What the hell is wrong with you?" Becca said. "I'm not leaving."

Why had he singled *her* out?

"Becca, I don't—" His face paled as he looked across the table. "Where's Sophie?"

"She went to answer the door." Amy pointed toward the open archway between the living room and dining room with a fork laden with roast. They had a clear view to the entry area.

"Buddy, what has gotten into you?" Mom said.

From the other room, Becca heard Sophie gasp, then say, "Oh my God."

Another wave of molten heat flooded through Becca. She pushed Buddy away, standing on her own and turning to face the front door. She could see Sophie, but not whoever was standing outside.

Dazzle ran back into the dining room and dove into her bed with a whimper. Pickles, though, was spinning in circles and barking excitedly. He usually only reacted that way to family.

The Pomeranian darted out the door and a booming male voice said, "Pickles! I've missed you, my fierce friend."

Whoever it was, he had a great voice. Deep and rumbly in a way that set Becca off even more than she already was.

The goosebumps escalated, tingles spreading through her in waves. Her mouth grew dry and she had to work to swallow.

Sophie was making half-formed sounds as she tried to speak. This guy must be something else, if he could render the chattiest of the siblings speechless.

"I am Kral," he said. "I'm here for Becca."

What the...?

"I'm... I'm Becca," Sophie stammered.

"No, she's not," Becca yelled. Of all the times to try that trick.

Even though they were born a year apart, Sophie and Becca were mistaken for twins all the time. Sophie sometimes used their similar appearances to fool people into thinking she was Becca to mess with them.

Becca had grown so tired of explaining that they just

had some strong genetics going on in their family that she didn't always bother to correct people. She was definitely going to in this case.

Amy also looked a lot like them, with the same dark hair and brown eyes that all the girls had. Thankfully, as the surprise addition to the family, she was ten years younger than Sophie, so no one mistook them for triplets.

"Right, I'm Sophie." Sophie leaned closer to the dining room so the door was blocking her face from the stranger's view. She turned to look at Becca, mouthing, "Oh my God," in a comically exaggerated way.

"Sophie, yes," the man—Kral—said. What the hell kind of name was *Kral*? "One of Buddy's other sisters."

Becca's heartbeat kicked up. She had trouble remembering to breathe. Her skin prickled into more goosebumps.

Hearing his voice made a very pleasant heat build deep in her belly and brought a strange ache to her chest. An ache she mercilessly stomped.

Men were trouble. Especially hot men. Becca got her fill of them on nights when she hung out with Amy at The Parched Flamingo where Amy tended bar. They had both listened to way too many victory stories from drunk guys talking about conquests—and seen too many women taken in by a gorgeous face or a smoking body. Judging by Sophie's reaction, this guy must be downright volcanic.

"May I enter?" Kral asked.

"Sure," Sophie said.

At the same time, Buddy yelled, "No, you may not."

Buddy let go of Becca's arm and started toward the door. Sophie was already opening it wider. Becca wanted to grab Buddy to stop him and tell him he was being rude, but she was frozen in place.

The man outside—because he was still outside— stepped into the house. He hadn't been blocked by the door. In fact Becca wasn't sure it could hide him if he tore it off the hinges and held the thing in front of him, which he looked absolutely capable of doing. The front door looked tiny next to him.

He ducked under the lintel, gripping it with one huge hand as if to help gauge how low it was compared to his head. Pickles was tucked against his chest, resting in the crook of Kral's arm and smiling like the happiest pup in the world.

Becca could hardly blame him.

Once Kral was inside, he stood. His entire head was above the height of the door. If he rose up on his toes, she was pretty sure he'd bonk the ceiling.

Sophie backed away a step, her eyes wide as she stared at him. He turned to shut the door, giving Becca a great view of his broad back, tight backside, and sculpted legs. The jeans he wore were so tight, she could see the lines of muscle pressing against the fabric.

Where the hell did he find clothes his size?

He wore metal wristbands that would have looked dorky on anyone else, but he somehow managed to pull off. They weren't quite chrome, but reflected the light almost as well.

His hair was more a mane of dark brown, broken into wavy strands with highlights like someone who spent most of their time in the ocean and sun. He turned around, revealing a full beard that completed the wild and windblown look. A necklace of shining, clear crystals rested on his chest, with some kind of amulet in the center.

With his shoulders hunched a bit, towering over Sophie, Becca should have found him menacing as hell. If a guy who looked like this walked into the sub shop when she was working, she would immediately be on high alert. Instead, more of that molten fire poured through her veins.

Kral looked over at her, his eyes a deep shade of orange that she'd never seen on anyone before. She swore he made a low, deep growl that she felt more than heard.

Then he was walking toward her and the rest of the world seemed to vanish. It was just her and this giant, hulking, gorgeous guy, falling toward each other like—

"Hey, Kral, this isn't a good time." Buddy stepped between them, breaking the spell.

Becca could finally move again. She used her newly recovered mobility to step to Buddy's side, which, unfortunately put her much closer to Kral. The hair on her arms stood on end, like he was putting out some kind of electrical field that was giving her all kinds of tingles.

"Don't be ridiculous," Kral said. "Time can neither be good nor bad. It simply is." He kept staring into Becca's eyes, even though he was speaking to Buddy.

"Oh, my," Mom said, her voice breathier than usual.

A broad smile broke out on Kral's face, his teeth gleaming brightly against his light brown skin. He finally broke eye contact, turning to walk over to their mom. He held up a small bouquet of wilted wildflowers.

"These are for you," he said.

Mom tittered. Becca had never heard anyone titter before, but she was sure that's what it sounded like. She could understand where it was coming from.

"Amy, run and get another place setting," Mom said.

"Don't bother." Buddy shook his head vigorously, but Amy was already on her way to the kitchen. "Kral was just leaving."

"But he just got here," Sophie whined.

"Nonsense." Dad stood up and patted Amy on the shoulder as she passed him. "We have a feast here. It'd be wrong not to share it."

"He can sit next to me," Sophie said.

Wow, Sophie was really calling dibs on the new guy. Which was nothing new.

What *was* new was the way the thought of Sophie claiming this guy set Becca's teeth on edge.

Amy returned from the kitchen with a plate, glass, and

utensils. She was even balancing an extra glass on the plate for the flowers. Mom rose from her seat to help get the extra place setting laid while Dad brought in an extra chair.

"It does smell spectacular," Kral said. "But then, your cooking has brought you fame throughout the galaxy." He laughed and slapped Buddy on the back, sending her "big" brother stumbling forward a few paces.

Buddy was usually the biggest person in the room. It was so weird to see him dwarfed by this guy.

Even weirder, her brother seemed almost desperate for Kral to leave. Becca had no idea why. Another secret. But this one, she had a chance to dig into.

"Come on, Buddy," she said, smirking. "We can't turn your friend away from your famous cooking."

She rested her hand on Kral's elbow, intending to steer him around the table to the spot between Amy and Sophie that they were already setting up. The moment her fingers touched his skin, the tingles she'd been feeling before amped up to full-on lightning strikes coursing along her nerve endings. She was almost dizzy from it.

Kral sucked in a quick breath, staring down at her again. His orange eyes seemed to glow. His lips twitched away from his teeth as his features took on a feral cast that made her toes curl.

He stepped closer, lifting a hand as if he meant to touch her face. She found herself wondering what it would be like to feel his huge hands tangled in her hair and—

"Okay, everything is ready." Sophie's sharp voice cut into the moment.

Becca stepped away from Kral, trying to steady her breathing. He kept that intense eye contact for a few moments, then turned and headed toward the opposite side of the table, where they'd set his place.

Sophie glared at Becca as they sat again. Becca couldn't bring herself to care. Her nerves were still lit up like a fireworks show.

Yeah, this guy was trouble with a capital 'T.'

Chapter Two

Kral could feel Becca's attention as she continued to stare at him with narrowed eyes from across the table. A scrutinizing stare.

The plates covering his spine kept trying to rise beneath his thin T-shirt. He forced them to stay against his back, not wanting to introduce Becca to that aspect of his alien nature quite yet.

What he *did* want to do was challenge someone to show her his prowess in battle. But there were no likely candidates nearby.

He thought of perhaps lifting the table and throwing it through the wall to show his strength. On Earth, such things were frowned upon. At least, that's what Vay had told him.

The Sadirian had been instructing Kral and his prism on the ways of Earthlings. She would not be pleased to know that Kral had snuck away from the group and flown half-way across the continent to meet Buddy's sister.

He had followed Vay's protocols by activating the holo-emitter that disguised the true color of his skin and hair. The Earthlings he had passed on his way to Becca's parents' house had stared, but that was probably more due to his size than anything else.

Risking Vay's anger was worth it to meet Becca. To feel her presence so close.

Her voice stirred him even more in person than it had when he'd first heard it over Buddy's communication device. Now that he had seen her, the strength in her gaze, the readiness in the way she carried herself, he was more drawn to her than ever.

Despite his distraction, he remembered to set Pickles on the floor when he reached his seat. Buddy had admonished Kral and his fellow Cygnian warriors repeatedly to not get the animal used to sitting in their laps while they ate. Pickles whined a bit, but then went to his soft bed where a similar animal rested.

"So, what are you, some kind of surfer dude?" Becca asked.

"Perhaps," Kral said. "I don't know what that is."

"A surfer?" The sister known as Sophie laughed and leaned closer to bump her shoulder against Kral's.

Becca's eyes narrowed further.

"Kral doesn't surf," Buddy said, his voice more serious than usual.

"But perhaps I should." Kral looked over to Becca. "Is it a challenging activity?"

"Only if you can't stay on the board," Becca said. "Or,

you know. You can't swim."

"*Swim.*" Kral hadn't heard that word and had no equivalent from his translator session.

"Kral's been in Kansas for a while," Buddy said. "I don't think he's had much of a chance to take in the scene here."

Kral took a bite of the protein Buddy had prepared. The meat melted on Kral's tongue, rich juices coating his mouth. He let out a groan of pleasure, his eyes rolling shut.

"Buddy, you have surpassed anything I've tasted before," Kral said. "Not even the delicacies of the Elythrian Core could compare."

"The what now?" Becca said.

"The beach isn't far from here." Sophie broke in with a strong voice, as if she was determined to keep the conversation on her topic of choice. "I'd be happy to take you." She leaned closer again. "The ocean is great this time of year."

"Ocean?" That was a word Kral had been taught since arriving. It was hard not to know it, with so much of the planet covered with the terrifying biome.

He wasn't sure how sentients interacted with liquid in such large areas. Why would they want to visit it? Even with the high sodium content of Earth's oceans, Kral and his fellow Cygnians would sink like the stones of their homeworld if they ever dared to venture into the waters.

"Don't tell me you've never been to the ocean," Sophie

said.

Kral smirked at her and bent his head closer, lowering his voice as he spoke. "All right, I won't."

He laughed as he straightened. Sisters were so much fun.

He couldn't wait to spend more time with his own newly-discovered sibling once she returned from her first visit to their home planet. A planet that did *not* have oceans, or any bodies of water, for that matter.

"What would we do at the ocean?" Kral asked.

Sophie's gaze softened and she let out a small cooing noise.

Across from him, Becca murmured, "Oh, brother."

When Buddy didn't respond, Kral said, "Buddy, I think Becca needs you for something."

"What?" Becca's lip had curled up and she was staring at Kral as if he had a Lyrian parcel in his hair.

He must be messing up the cultural mores again. But he had distinctly heard her call for her brother.

Rather than make matters worse, he turned back to Sophie and cast a broad smile at her, hoping she would pick up their earlier conversation. He wasn't disappointed.

"I mostly sunbathe," Sophie said. "But there are lots of nice guys who can teach you how to surf."

"Sophie's dated most of them," Amy said, from his other side.

"Amy," their father warned.

"Dated." Kral knew the term wasn't about marking time. That was obvious from the context. But he wasn't sure what it could mean.

"Can you blame her?" Their mother laughed. "You know, your father was quite the surfer back in the day."

"That was a while ago," their father replied.

The pair cast gazes at each other filled with love and the intimate knowledge only shared by true bondmates. Kral felt pressure build in his chest, his hearts shifting closer to a matching beat.

He wanted that bond. But with Cygnians, it was so unlikely. Their female population was less than a tenth of their total numbers.

When he'd heard Becca speak—when her voice had lifted in song—the sound had called to him as none ever had before. It gave him hope where he should have none.

She was an Earthling, after all.

Nuar, another member of his prism, swore that he had achieved a soulmate bond with an Earthling named Lian. Observing them, it was obvious they belonged together. But were they truly soulmates?

"Kral doesn't surf," Buddy said. "He can't swim."

"What do you mean, I *can't*?" Kral said. There was no physical activity that a Cygnian couldn't do—least of all Kral, their crown prince.

The slight brought his attention fully back to Buddy. Kral slammed his hands on the table as he rose to his feet, barely remembering in time to pull back his strength when he struck the soft wood. Even so, all the dishes bounced with loud clatters. His chair fell over backward.

Their mother put a hand to her chest and said, "Oh, dear."

Buddy was impressively unfazed. Then again, he'd been spending quite a bit of time with Kral and his prism and had shown a great ability to handle himself among the Cygnian warriors.

"Kral, to surf, you have to get into the ocean," Buddy said. "You paddle a tiny board far out from shore, then stand on it as you ride it back on a giant wave. And you try not to fall off the board. Into the water. Into the *deep* water." Buddy took another bite, and mumbled, "And did I mention you're far from the shore?"

"I see," Kral said.

He could use the technology in his wristbands to create an air pocket around himself with recirculated gases fit for his physiology, but perhaps Buddy didn't know that.

Kral would also still have to walk along the bottom of the ocean to return to the shore. Depending on the depth, there might be insufficient light to power his wristbands for long.

That was not a scenario he wished to contemplate.

There would be other challenges, as well. His blue skin and hair were easily covered by his holo-emitter so that he could walk amongst Earthlings unobtrusively as he did now. Explaining how he could survive beneath the water for such a long time would be a bigger problem.

"I accept your point." Kral picked up his chair and sat back down. He took another bite of the delicious feast.

"Wait, what the hell was that?" Becca said. "You don't pound on the table and knock over a chair and then act as if nothing happened. And so much of what you guys are talking about doesn't even make sense."

"Kral can't swim," Buddy said.

"He's right." Kral nodded. "My body is too dense."

"He'd sink like a stone." Buddy shuddered. Kral would have to reassure his friend later.

"Muscle mass *is* denser and you have plenty of that." Sophie reached over and squeezed Kral's bicep. "Oh my God. You're like rock solid. Are you flexing?"

"Sophie," their mom said, swatting at Sophie's shoulder.

Amy rolled her eyes and Becca let out a disgusted snort.

Kral wasn't sure what had prompted the admonishments. There was much about this conversation he himself didn't understand.

But he wanted to. He desperately wanted to.

"Sisters are quite something, are they not?" Kral said, angling his head somewhat toward Becca.

"I'll say," she said.

"I discovered that I have a sister not long ago." Kral

smiled as he thought of Sorca.

"Was she adopted or something?" Becca asked.

Her interest warmed Kral's hearts and he felt his smile deepen.

"No, she was created in—"

Buddy cleared his throat loudly. "It was a sperm bank...type...situation."

For some reason, Buddy's face turned bright red. He coughed, then quickly drank some of his water.

Becca put down her utensils, turned in her seat to face Buddy, rested her elbow on the table, and propped her head against her hand.

"Sperm bank?" she said.

"His dad...made a contribution," Buddy said.

"What's a sperm bank?" Kral asked.

Buddy coughed again. "I'll explain later." He gulped more of his water. "Actually, you know what? I'm gonna let someone else explain that one."

"Let me get this straight." Becca turned her attention back to Kral, though she kept her arm resting on the table. "You don't know what surfing is. Or swimming. Or sperm banks."

"Becca," their mother whispered.

Becca continued without pause. "My brother gets another of his 'mysterious calls' on his new high-tech watch—that probably cost more than this house—then you show up right after looking like..." She gestured at Kral, sweeping her hand up and down. "*That.*"

Kral paused in his eating. He leaned a bit closer to the youngest sister, Amy. "Is something wrong with my appearance?"

"Not at all," Sophie said, from his other side.

Amy shook her head and rolled her eyes, a habit Kral noticed she and Becca shared. Amy didn't say anything, but kept eating her own delicious meal.

"I want to know what the hell is going on," Becca said.

"Language!" their mother said.

"Yeah, Becca," Amy said. "No swearing at the table."

Becca scowled at Amy, then turned her piercing stare back to Kral. His skin prickled under her gaze, his hearts beating faster and stronger. The cadence edged closer to unity—closer to a matching beat than he'd ever experienced before.

He needed to fight something. To show her his prowess. To let her know he could protect her and match her fierceness in battle.

Kral shook himself inwardly. These thoughts were reserved for one's bondmate. There was no way a human should be eliciting them.

Could Nuar be right about his union with Lian? Were their soulmates here, on Earth?

If so, the future of his *people* was here. The future of all Cygnians. Kral had to know, one way or another.

Kral wasn't the only one chasing a mystery. Becca

seemed just as intent on learning more about Kral.

"Who *are* you?" Becca said.

That answer was simple enough. "I am Kral, son of Ehmach and Korvin, crown—"

"He's my friend, and he's answered enough of your questions," Buddy cut in before Kral could finish his litany of titles. "Could we please just eat?"

Kral studied Buddy as silence fell over the table. The meal was truly amazing, but it was hard to enjoy it fully while distracted by so many things that didn't make sense.

Kral's reaction to Becca was mystery enough, but how Buddy's family was reacting to Kral... It was almost as if they had no idea Kral was from another planet. But why would Buddy keep that secret?

He was involved with a Sadirian. Surely, he had let his family know of Nika's origins.

And yet, the more Kral thought over the conversation —as well as more he'd had in the past with Buddy—the more certain he became that his family was ignorant of such matters. Important matters.

"You haven't told them," Kral said, the answer to this one mystery at last becoming clear.

"Told us what?" Becca's eyes lit up as she glanced between Kral and Buddy.

"About me," Kral said. "My prism and the others."

"Are you really into crystals or something?" Sophie asked.

Kral laughed. If they could see his homeworld, they would be in awe. The entire planet was covered in crystalline formations. The Cygnians had perfected the art of growing crystals into whatever form they needed—even into spaceships.

And the planet itself was surrounded by a great sphere of crystal that protected every life form on the planet from the harshest effects of the radiation and gravity waves from the nearby black hole. The Cygnians had still evolved to be incredibly strong and resilient. Everything on the planet needed to be in order to survive.

Had Buddy truly not shared anything he had learned of the universe with his family? Not about other sentients beyond their solar system or—more importantly—the ones colonizing the Sol system and Earth itself?

"Buddy," Kral began. "You need to tell them. Keeping them unaware isn't safe."

Buddy dropped his utensils, shaking his head and lowering his gaze. He shook his head, then said, "You don't get to tell me how to keep my family safe."

He looked up at Kral, his eyes bright with fury. Buddy slammed his fist on the table, adding, "You shouldn't be here."

"Hey," five voices said in unison.

Becca stood up. With a tone full of command, she said, "Take it outside!"

"Take what outside?" Kral looked around the table,

trying to see what she wanted him to remove.

"Your argument," she said. "You and Buddy both. Outside. Now."

Buddy stood and strode from the room. He opened the door and waited, glaring at Kral through the large open archway that separated the dining hall from the living area.

Kral stood and carefully made his way to the other side of the table.

"I thank you for your hospitality," he said. "And didn't mean to disrupt your meal."

"It's all right," their mother said. "Buddy shouldn't have talked to you that way. Neither should Becca."

"Mom," Becca said.

"You grilled him like a suspect in a crime show." Amy picked up her plate and started toward the kitchen. "Speaking of which, I'm heading home to finish binge-watching my new favorite before my shift at the bar later."

"It's good to have priorities," Sophie said, then snorted.

"I'm glad to have met you all," Kral said.

"And you as well." Their mother's cheeks pinked as she smiled at him.

"Kral," Becca said, sharply. "Outside. I mean it."

The skin along his back bristled at her challenge. The protective plates that covered his spine shivered, wanting to rise. He kept them clamped down.

Few dared to speak to him that way. He walked over to her, looming above her. She didn't back down a bit, glaring at him with her rich brown eyes.

Kral smiled, then turned and joined Buddy at the door.

When Sophie moved to stand, Becca pointed at her sharply, and said, "You stay."

Sophie scowled, but settled back into her seat.

Becca herded them outside, shutting the door behind them.

Chapter Three

"Becca, this is between Kral and me," Buddy said. "Go back inside."

"Not happening." Becca had been shut out entirely too long and she was sick of it.

Kral's eyebrows lifted, but he said nothing. Smart guy.

"I want to know what this is all about," Becca demanded. "And I'm not going to accept, 'Oh, he's in love!' Or 'He's sorting out how to balance a relationship with his family,' or any of that bullshit."

"You have no idea what you're talking about," Buddy said.

Becca let out an exasperated breath. "Of course I don't. Because you refuse to tell me anything! You've never kept me in the dark before, and it's driving me crazy. I know there's way more going on than just a new relationship."

"Becca…" Buddy's shoulders sagged, but he didn't deny it.

"You should tell her the truth," Kral said.

"You should have stayed in Harbor." Buddy pointed aggressively at Kral, which really didn't seem like a good idea.

Sure, her brother could handle himself in a fight, and if it came down to it she'd side with him. But Kral looked like he could flatten them both without breaking a sweat.

Weirdly, the idea of fighting Kral made her stomach ache. When she looked at him, more of those goosebumps shimmered down her spine.

Lucky for them, Kral just stood there calmly as her brother paced back and forth. Buddy ran his hands through his hair, then blew out a breath.

"Okay. Truth," he said.

Becca's heart was in her throat. Finally, some answers.

Her arm twitched. She realized that she was reaching for Kral's hand just in time to stop herself. What was up with *that*?

"You know Brendan Sloan, the genius who gave me this watch?" Buddy held up his wrist, as if she'd forgotten what the fancy thing looked like, with its blank silver face and sturdy black band.

"Yeah, Nika's boss," Becca said.

Buddy let out a sigh. "He's not Nika's boss. I keep telling you that. But he works with her. And he also..." Buddy took another deep breath. He glanced over at Kral before continuing. "He also used to work for the government. On super secret stuff. Like top-level classified."

"Okay." Becca wasn't that surprised.

Buddy's watch was really advanced, from what Becca could tell. And the few times Nika had visited, she'd had similar gadgets. Dad was still gushing about how Nika had fixed up the old hatchback in a single day when he'd been tinkering with it for decades and never got it to start. He said it ran smoother than the latest cars off the line now.

Becca had hung out with Nika for a bit while she was working on the car, trying to get information out of her. Asking questions hadn't worked, but Becca had seen Nika's equipment do some weird stuff—lasers coming from screwdrivers and "magnets" summoning parts from across the room.

Once, Becca had even sworn she'd seen the engine block floating a few inches above the car. Buddy had been there and ushered Becca out before she could get a closer look.

So, yeah. Classified government work sounded about right.

"Why didn't you just tell me?" Becca said. "You could have said this right away, and I would have let it be."

That he hadn't done so made her suspect there was still more that he wasn't telling her. Things that he actually *could* tell her, but was deciding not to. This felt more like him throwing her a bone to get her off his back than actually sharing anything real.

"I didn't tell you because Nika and Brendan are both involved in some dangerous stuff," Buddy said. "They're trying to keep me out of it as much as they can. I've asked them to, so that you all don't get sucked up in it."

Becca laughed. She couldn't help it.

"How could we possibly get involved in all that?" she said. "I run the sub shop with you—or mostly instead of you lately." He winced, and she almost regretted the jab. "Amy's a bartender, Sophie's a dog trainer, and mom and dad are retired. She was a nurse and he was in sales. We're not exactly in positions to affect national security. Or any kind of security."

Buddy lifted his arms, then let them drop to his sides. "I can't explain more."

Kral let out a disgusted grunt. He stepped closer to Buddy, moving fast and with his hands fisted.

Becca's heart leapt into her throat again. She'd seen this aggressive posturing too many times. But if Kral went for Buddy—like really went for him—she doubted her brawling skills would be enough, even with Buddy's help.

Thankfully, Kral didn't take a swing. He settled for getting right up in her brother's space, towering over his own six-foot something height.

"You *can* explain more," Kral said. "You're choosing not to."

Just as Becca had suspected.

Buddy didn't back down. Becca wasn't sure if she was proud of his gutsiness or convinced he was an idiot. Probably a little of both. Kral was a full foot taller than him.

"I'm doing what I need to do to keep them safe," Buddy said.

"Ignorance is a security risk," Kral said.

"Oh, that's great." Buddy's voice dripped with sarcasm. "Quoting Dorn at me now?"

Who was Dorn? Becca filed the name away for later.

"I'm trying to get you to see reason," Kral said. "There are things happening on your planet that are dangerous to ignore."

Wait, '*your planet?*' Kral talked as if it wasn't his as well.

"Your family could easily get swept up in dangerous events whether they realize it or not," Kral continued. "Being aware of the risks gives them more options for action. They need to know what's going on to keep themselves safe."

"Getting involved makes them more of a target." Buddy stepped forward, miraculously closing even more of the tiny space between the two men. Their chests were practically brushing. "I'm not backing down on this. Respect my ways as I've always respected yours."

Kral shook his head. "Brother…" he said. "For the first time, you disappoint me."

Buddy's eyebrows creased and a stricken look crossed his features. He opened his mouth briefly, but then snapped it shut, his lips tightening.

She'd been so close to getting answers, but Becca felt like all she had were more questions. Worse, she felt as though Buddy had been hurt by her pushing.

Kral had called him "brother." So, this was another new BFF.

I am not being replaced. Even though apparently he now confides in all these other people instead of me.

If her brother was widening his social circle, good for him. But still, what the hell was going on here?

Whatever it was, the feeling that he was leaving her behind grew stronger with every little snippet of information she managed to get.

"I will leave," Kral said. "But this is not over."

Kral stepped to the side rather than backing away. He bowed slightly toward Becca, then turned and walked off.

Becca took a few steps after him before she realized what she was doing. Even after she managed to stop, she found herself leaning in his direction.

She wanted to run after him and had no idea why. The goosebumps that had been running down her spine since just before Kral showed up were painfully intense.

Buddy shouted, "Kral? What's not over? Kral?"

Buddy's watch beeped again. Becca was grateful for the distraction. She needed to get herself under control.

"Dammit," Buddy said. He brought his wrist nearer to his face and slammed the surface of the watch. "What?" he shouted.

"I... Uh..." A female voice came from the watch, crystal clear. And it wasn't Nika. The woman cleared her throat and squeaked out, "Is everything okay?"

Becca felt bad for whoever it was. Buddy had jumped down her throat.

"Yeah, everything's fine," Buddy said, deflating. "Sorry, Vay. I didn't mean to snap."

He looked up and stared at Becca as if he was surprised to find her still standing there. She crossed her arms and glared at him.

Buddy's mouth tightened and he let out a long breath through his nose. "Look, Vay, this isn't a good time," he said. "Kral is on his way back to Harbor. I have to smooth things over with my family."

"Oh, no," Vay said. "Did he make it inside your house?"

"Yeah," Buddy said.

"I'm sorry I didn't warn you sooner." She picked up speed as she spoke, kind of like Sophie, only a lot more focused. "I called you the moment I discovered he wasn't here. With how much interest he's expressed in meeting your family, especially Becca, I figured that's where he'd gone. Do you need me to dispatch a team to—"

"Vay," Buddy broke in. "Becca is standing right next to me."

There was a long pause. "Oh."

Becca leaned forward and said, "And she's really

interested in knowing why Kral was so interested in meeting her."

"Uh…" Vay said.

Buddy let out a sigh. "I'll call you back later, Vay. And no, I don't need a team. But thanks for asking."

"Okay," she squeaked.

Buddy tapped the watch, then let his arms drop to his sides. They stared at each other for several long moments.

"So?" he finally said. "What are you going to grill me about first?"

Becca could hardly pick a topic. There had been so many new possibilities opened up by that call. And every single piece of information she'd gained just gave her more questions.

She decided to start with, "What kind of team was Vay offering to send exactly?"

And what was up with the weird names?

Buddy shook his head. "I'm honestly not sure. With Vay, it's always kind of a crapshoot."

His mouth twitched on one side, like he wanted to smile. Whoever Vay was, Becca was sure Buddy would call her another of his new friends.

"You've been really busy lately," Becca said.

"I know, but I make it to family dinner and I come around the shop as much as I—"

"That's not what I meant." Becca paused, formulating her thoughts. "The sub shop used to be your life. Now, you've practically handed it over to me. You're letting other people run the place when I'm not there."

"They can handle it."

"I'm not saying they can't. I'm saying you never would have given them a chance to before Nika. I thought—we all thought—she's what this was all about. That you were spending all your time with her."

He let out a snort. "I wish. She's so busy, I'm lucky if I get to see her a couple nights a month."

"Buddy…" As mad as Becca was, she knew her brother was absolutely smitten with Nika. It must be hell for him to have to be apart from her. "Can't she make time for—"

Buddy cut in. "Her work is important. Like 'lives depending on her' important." He shook his head, his eyes losing focus. "So many lives."

Becca reached for Buddy's hand and squeezed it.

"I've been trying to go visit her more," he said. "She's splitting her time between so many projects, we don't get that much time together even when I do. And I'm trying to stay close to home."

"Buddy…" Becca didn't know what else to say. Suddenly, her curiosity seemed so selfish. She hadn't realized how much her brother was struggling.

At least he wasn't alone. She was suddenly grateful he had a bunch of new friends.

"That Kral guy seemed to really like you," Becca said. "Did Nika introduce you?"

Buddy laughed. "I suppose you could say that. Remember how I told you I was gonna surprise her with a Solstice feast last year since I didn't know what she celebrated?"

"I remember." Becca smiled as she recalled the conversation—and how she'd cajoled her brother into telling Nika how he really felt.

"Well, I…" He paused as if he was trying to figure out what he should and shouldn't share. "She was called in to work, and I kind of hid in her truck with the dinner in a picnic basket."

Becca's smile broadened. She could just see Buddy hunkered down in the back of Nika's shiny covered pick-up, a basket tucked under his arm.

"Did it work?" Becca asked.

"Oh yeah." His eyes widened and became unfocused again. "I popped out of the truck right in the middle of…" He shook his head. "Something I had no business being in the middle of."

Becca was dying to know more, but she didn't want to push him. She squeezed his hand instead of prying.

"That's how I met Kral." Buddy pointed in the direction the giant had taken.

Wait, where was Kral's car? Had he *walked* from somewhere?

Becca turned to look down the street and didn't see any vehicles she didn't recognize. But Buddy was still talking.

There was no way she was going to distract him now that he was opening up.

"There was a misunderstanding," Buddy said. "Believe it or not, you and Sophie and Amy and Mom singing that four-part harmony holiday music saved the day."

Becca snorted before she could stop herself. When Buddy looked at her, she said, "Come on. Seriously?"

"I wouldn't joke about you guys's singing."

Buddy kept a straight face for about five seconds before finally giving her a real smile. Becca realized she hadn't seen it in a long time. Damn, she'd been too absorbed in her own stuff.

"That's why Kral wanted to meet you," Buddy said. "He and his pals, they were really impressed with your singing."

"Why did he want to meet me in particular, though?"

Kral had specifically asked about Becca when he'd arrived. Even Vay had mentioned Becca. Not Sophie, not Amy, not Mom.

Buddy looked away and rubbed the back of his neck. She was definitely pushing him again and needed to back off.

"I don't know," he said. "I guess he liked the sound of your voice in particular."

Right, like he'd be able to pick out Becca's voice from a four-part harmony.

She didn't press the matter. Instead, she bumped

Buddy's shoulder with hers and said, "Maybe he liked that I gave you crap when you first called."

Buddy laughed. "Yeah, probably. That sounds like Kral."

She laughed along with him. The next silence they shared was a lot more comfortable. She hoped it was comforting as well.

"I'll stop pushing," she said. "About Nika, about where you run off to. About all of it."

Buddy's shoulders actually dropped as he let out a breath, like a weight had fallen from them.

"And I'll cover for you with the family," she added.

"That'd really help."

"But you have to promise me something."

His expression became a little guarded again, so she hurried on.

"Promise me that you'll remember that I'm here for you," she said. "If you need someone to talk to—as much as you're able. Or if you just want to have a beer in silence. I'm here."

He nodded, then pulled her into a big hug.

She'd missed this. Missed him. But now that she understood a little better what he was dealing with, she would suck it up and be the sister he needed her to be.

Chapter Four

Kral piloted his small craft over the flat plains of Kansas, heading toward the newest Department of Homeworld Security base. This one was an entire town that they had colonized, bringing the people who lived there into their trust.

Earthlings and their secrets. Kral didn't understand it, but hiding certain truths seemed an important part of their society. Perhaps if he was as fragile as these life forms, he would keep more to himself as well.

Harbor came into view. Kral headed toward the small airfield just west of the town, dropping his cloak as he neared the hangar that had been set aside for the ship he and his prism had arrived in. Green prairie grass parted in his wake as he approached the enormous building in his crystalline vessel.

Rather than reintegrate his shard with the *Arrow*, he landed next to the main ship. He could see people waiting for him to disembark.

Lar was there, as Kral expected. Vay was there, too, which he had not.

This would be interesting.

The bottom of his shard opened up to form a ramp, angling so that he could slide easily from the small fighter. The end of the ramp remained a few feet off the ground. He turned as he slid, landing on his feet and hopping up to greet the odd pair before him.

Lar's dark skin was a rich cobalt hue and his eyes gleamed yellow. His midnight-blue hair was braided into thick locks that fell far past his shoulders. He wasn't quite as tall as Kral, but still stood a foot taller than the Sadirian woman beside him.

Seeing them side-by-side was almost comical. She was so thin, Kral wondered if a strong wind might blow her over. Her skin was pale and her short-cut hair a light gold. She seemed to be avoiding his gaze with her bright blue eyes.

Kral lifted his arm and Lar stepped forward to strike his wristband against Kral's. The sound echoed through the hangar, vibrating against Kral's skin and bringing the air around them to life.

Vay curled her hands into fists and held them up at the sides of her chest in a Cygnian gesture, then bowed her head. "Your highness," she said, an odd, crisp note to her tone.

Kral pulled himself up to his full height, angling his head so he could stare down his nose at her. He used a ridiculously imperious voice as he said, "I've commanded that you not use that title while I am on Earth."

Vay stammered a bit, mumbling an apology. She still wouldn't meet his eyes.

"I… It's just…" she began. "You're the crown prince. A certain level of respect is mandated."

Lar leaned closer to her and said, "He's messing with you again."

Vay snapped her mouth shut and cast a withering glare at Kral. He burst out laughing and wrapped one arm over her shoulders, gently squeezing her against his side.

"I know there's fire in you," he said. "And I can take it. Go ahead. Light into me."

She took a deep breath and began, her voice a bit shaky. "Your…" This time, she caught herself. "*Kral*. I thought you understood that your group is to remain in Harbor. If you'd like to tour more of the planet, I'd be happy to arrange it."

Polite to the last.

He wondered what it would take to make the Sadirian cultural liaison breach etiquette and actually smack him. That would be something.

"You know, I was very entertained by your greeting— before you used the title," he said, ignoring her comment. "I never thought I'd see a Sadirian taking an interest in Cygnian culture."

"Of course I'm interested," she said, exasperation flooding her voice. "This is an amazing opportunity for our people to build strong connections and learn about each other. And your culture is absolutely fascinating. Rom has been teaching me a great deal—"

"Rom?" Kral said.

"Well, yes." Vay blinked as if she wasn't sure what the issue was.

"Be careful around that one," Lar said. "He's a… What do the Earthlings say? A heart-breaker."

Vay's nose crinkled as if she'd smelled something repugnant. Perhaps this would be a way to rile her up. Kral had never met anyone as agreeable as Vay. He loved the challenge of trying to goad her.

Besides that, he could sense an underlying stress in the woman. She did everything in her power to please everyone around her in her role as liaison between the aliens and Earthlings cohabitating in the small town. It had to be a burden. He wanted her to know she could cut loose with him and his prism if she needed—or wanted—to.

Again he wondered at the situation. He had never thought he'd meet a Sadirian that he would grow to care about.

"Rom is very aware that I have a bondmate," Vay said.

Lar lifted his eyebrows. "Indeed."

"I assure you, he's been nothing but polite to me," Vay said.

Kral nodded as if deep in thought. "Perhaps he's holding back because your bondmate's adopted parents are

Lyrians."

The huge, four-armed aliens were one of the few sentients in the galaxy who could rival the Cygnians in sturdiness and strength. It was fascinating that a mated pair had adopted an Earthling.

What is it about this planet?

"I don't think they'd take kindly to someone else 'putting the moves' on you," Lar said.

"What moves?" Kral asked. "Fighting moves?"

Lar shook his head. "It's another Earth expression."

Kral laughed. "Do these people speak in anything besides idioms?"

"Gentlemen," Vay said, lifting her hands emphatically. "If we could stay on topic."

"I have no idea what topic you mean," Kral said. "This conversation has been delightfully varied."

A muscle in Vay's cheek leapt. He could practically hear her teeth grind together.

So close...

"About you remaining in Harbor," she said. "There are protocols in place for travel to ensure that unauthorized Earthlings don't find out about our presence."

"Then you have nothing to worry about." Kral gave her shoulders another squeeze, being careful not to press too tight. "I didn't visit any unauthorized Earthlings."

"Oh." She looked vaguely confused. "Well, that's good."

He dropped his arm from her and walked toward his ship. Lar fell in step beside him.

"I just visited Buddy's family," Kral said.

Her mouth dropped open. "You *what?*"

Kral and Lar paused and looked back at Vay, then threw their heads back and laughed. Vay's cheeks turned pink.

"Very funny," she said, crossing her arms. "You nearly gave me a stomach attack."

Lar composed himself and said, "I believe the Earth expression is 'a heart attack.'"

"Thank you." She turned her attention back to Kral. "I must ask you to refrain from making any more unaccompanied trips around the planet."

Kral bowed low. "Of course. I swear to you, I will not make any more unaccompanied trips around the planet during this visit."

Vay's eyebrows furrowed, but she nodded and bowed in return. He should probably tell her that bowing was him messing with her and not something that his people often did. Vay's curiosity about the Cygnians was as expansive as her knowledge of them was limited—not surprising, given her Sadirian background.

"If you would excuse us, I have things to discuss with Lar," Kral said.

"Oh, of course." She gave him one last bow. "Please don't hesitate to call for me if you need anything this evening."

"You are most kind," Kral said.

Vay half-smiled, then turned and headed from the hangar. Kral and Lar watched her depart, then stood in silence for several more moments.

Finally, Lar said, "Did you find the answers you sought?"

Kral shook his head. "Only more questions."

"Come then. Let's discuss them." Lar clapped Kral's back, hard enough to push him forward a step.

Kral grinned as he turned to his friend. It was nice to be around beings who wouldn't break if Kral bumped into them too hard.

Lar's forehead scrunched up. "You look odd in their hue."

"Right." Kral struck his wristbands together with a clang.

A wave of vibration rippled over his skin. The hologram cloaking his true appearance deactivated, revealing his blue skin and hair.

His eyes always remained orange. Even if their scientists could create a hologram strong enough to cover their vibrant light, it would go against everything in their Cygnian nature to use it.

Earthlings had another expression that Kral was very fond of. "The eyes are the windows to the soul." For Kral's people, the quote carried truth.

"That's more like it," Lar said. "I know we need to keep up our cover while out among Earthlings, but I'd just as soon see our prism as we truly are when we're with each other."

"Agreed." Kral clamped his hand on Lar's shoulder briefly, not bothering to mute his strength.

They turned toward the *Arrow* hovering above them and watched as the circular hatch in the bottom of the ship opened. Lights reflected off its crystal hull, projecting rainbows on the hangar walls. Once the hatch opened fully, they leapt the twenty feet up into the belly of the ship, landing on the edge of the lowest level of the ship.

Dorn stood nearby, arms crossed over his massive chest. His long, pale hair was tied back from his forehead, but otherwise left to its own, falling around his shoulders.

Unlike most of the others, who periodically disembarked from the ship, he was wearing a standard Cygnian uniform—a white tunic and leather breaches in the same color. He also wore a blaster in a holster at his belt that was strapped to his thigh.

Kral knew there were several other weapons hidden around his person. Dorn took his position as head of security very seriously.

"Dorn," Lar said, nodding briefly as they passed the Cygnian warrior.

Dorn angled his head in response, but said nothing. He pressed the control panel that closed the hatch behind them.

Kral glanced back over his shoulder. "Am I the last to return then?"

"Rom visited the town earlier," Lar said. "He took Bron with him, but they returned several hours ago. The rest of us stayed close to the ship in case you needed us."

Kral arched an eyebrow at him.

"Although we knew it would be completely unnecessary," Lar added.

Kral laughed. "And Nuar?"

"Ah yes." Lar was quiet for a few moments. "He's here, though he has been spending most of his time with Lian and her family. He still insists that she is his soulmate."

"And you still don't believe him," Dorn said from behind them as they travelled up the sloped, curving hallway that led to the common room.

"I believe that he wants to believe it," Lar said. "We all do. But Cygnians do not mate with non-Cygnians."

"And thus, we become extinct," Dorn said.

"Our people will not die out," Kral said. "Regardless of our population imbalance. We will find a way to survive."

Once they reached the common room, Kral struck his wristbands together and hummed the note that would activate the ship's central holographic display. A miniature image of Harbor appeared in the center of the room, so lifelike, they could make out the features of people walking down the street in minute detail.

Each sentient was surrounded by an aura that identified their species. Bright blue for Lyrians, orange for Antareans, green for Vegans, and yellow for the Earthlings and Sadirians—their scans still couldn't tell them apart.

At least no unknowns appeared. The Vegans had tightened security since a Scorpiian was discovered in town, undoubtedly hunting down some bounty or another. Earth's resources had already begun to draw unsavory types.

Kral pushed the thought from his mind and focused on all that was good about Harbor.

"This entire town has been set up as a place where sentients can visit Earth and learn about their many cultures and how they coexist, as well as sharing our culture with the humans living here," Kral said. "Everyone in Harbor knows they aren't the only intelligent life forms that exist in the universe."

"A handful of people on an otherwise ignorant planet," Lar said.

"A miraculous display of sentients working together," Kral retorted. "Helping each other. Lyrians live among Antareans. Sadirians work by their side. And the Vegans…"

He shook his head, still having trouble believing the legendary reptilian humanoids were real, let alone that they were with him in this small Earth town.

"The Vegans are here," he said. "And that gives me hope. There is a reason we have all been drawn to Earth. I intend to discover what that reason is."

"Kral!" Nuar called out to Kral as he entered the common room, followed by the rest of the prism.

Nuar walked over and lifted his arm. Kral struck his wristband and a wave of sound flowed through the room. The walls vibrated with the frequency, colors racing across the crystalline surface.

"It's good to have you back." Rom said, gripping Kral's shoulder and squeezing it.

Tarn and Bron sat at the table where they'd been playing a long game of Shimmer. The tiles adhered to the table so that they wouldn't lose their place, even if something managed to shake the ship. The tiles were more likely to be disrupted by their roughhousing, honestly.

"Speaking of the Vegans, look at this." Lar held up his wristband and activated its imaging function.

A three-dimensional projection appeared of him standing next to a huge, white-furred Lyrian. It looked like they were standing in front of the chocolate shop on Harbor's Main Street.

The Lyrian had one of his four arms wrapped around Lar's shoulders. With another, he was holding up a reptilian humanoid, presumably so the tiny creature could be in the picture with them. The Vegan didn't look very happy about it.

Rom shook his head. "I can't believe you're still going on about the Vegans."

"We only just discovered they're real," Lar said. "Didn't your parents ever tell you stories about the Vegans?"

"Mine did," Tarn said. "It's why I became an engineer." He slid a tile into a different position and Bron let out a low growl.

"This one is named Periwinkle," Lar said. "He let me take a selfie with him."

"Selfie?" Kral asked.

"It's an Earth expression for a picture of oneself taken at moments that have little cultural significance, but do have personal importance," Lar said.

"Actually, it's only a selfie if you take it yourself," Rom said. "Otherwise, it's just a commemorative photo."

"Photo…" Lar said, his lip curling up as he said the strange word. "But if I had tried to take this myself, my data processors couldn't have captured us all together."

"Which is why I took it for you," Nuar said.

"This is a selfie." Rom activated the imaging function on his wristband. A picture of his face right next to an Earth woman appeared above it, their cheeks mashed together.

"That looks uncomfortable," Lar said.

Rom laughed. "Oh, trust me, we made each other very comfortable. I have to say, the females on Earth are certainly welcoming." Rom headed to the bench that ran along one wall of the common room.

"I still don't understand why the Vegans would choose a low-tech planet like this for their new home," Lar said.

Kral wondered about that as well. Earth certainly had appeal, with the vast variety of ecosystems, life forms, and resources, but still...

There were millions of planets and colonies scattered throughout the galaxy who would welcome the Vegans as kings and queens. Planets filled with sentients who already knew there were many different intelligent forms of life traveling through the stars and wouldn't be shocked to find another among their number.

Most Earthlings had no idea they weren't alone in the universe. From what Kral had read of the planet's many cultures, they might not react well to the knowledge— hence the Department of Homeworld Security keeping everything secret.

"As long as the Vegans call Earth their home, this planet will be protected by the most technologically advanced beings in the galaxy," Bron said. "No one will dare bring it into the war."

At last, Dorn entered the conversation. "Someone already has. Lian was kidnapped."

"By a single rogue agent," Lar said.

"A rogue agent working with the Tau Ceti and who had possession of a Centauran ship," Nuar said, clearly agitated to be reminded of how close he'd come to losing Lian.

Nuar continued, "A rogue agent who implied that he had a working blue space drive, even though this ship was much too small to fit one of any design we're familiar with. He would have succeeded in taking Lian as well as the Lyrian infant he'd abducted for his sick studies had it not been for our soulmate bond."

Lar shook his head and looked away.

Again, Kral wondered why Lar was so adamant that Nuar and Lian couldn't have a true soulmate bond. Yes, she wasn't a Cygnian, but if their people were going to have a chance at survival, they had to start looking outside of their planet for mates. It was a blessing that Earth might be providing those mates, yet Lar vehemently opposed even considering the idea.

"For better or worse, you have begun the process of allying us with Earth," Lar said.

Kral could feel the multi-colored gazes of his prism upon him—a full spectrum of Cygnian Warriors. Warriors who had followed Kral to this comparatively primitive planet without question.

"I met Becca." Kral felt every man in the room hold their breath, waiting. But he wasn't sure what to say.

They knew Becca's voice had moved him when he heard her sing along with her sisters. Even through Buddy's phone and across the vast distance between

Cygnian space—where they had been—and Earth, her voice had caused a vibration within Kral's hearts, his mind, his body.

In that moment, his heartbeats had shifted toward unity. He'd never experienced anything like it before.

But he'd heard tales.

Frequency. The unique experience of being exposed to his soul's other half—made all the more rare with how few Cygnian females existed.

Kral had never dreamed he would achieve frequency with someone. If he had dared to dream, it would have been with another Cygnian, not someone from Earth.

But she was here. And she was his.

It didn't make any sense.

"You met the woman whose voice moved you," Bron said.

Kral nodded.

"And when you were in her presence?" Bron continued. "Was there a similar effect?"

How could Kral explain? And how could he dare to raise the hopes of his prism—that they, too, might find their souls' other halves here on this planet—until he was certain?

Prisms were made up of Cygnians whose souls formed a unique harmony. Only one set of people would ever match as well as Kral did with these six men, his brothers in everything but blood. The fact that he'd found them so early in his life and found a full spectrum was almost unheard of.

He was already so fortunate. It seemed wrong that he should also find his mate. Everything about this was wrong.

Except for Becca.

"It was indescribable," Kral said. "My hearts pounded in her presence. My skin felt electrified. My bones shook with every sound of her voice, urging me to take her into my arms."

"And did you?" Nuar asked, stepping closer.

"Of course not." Kral strode away and began pacing back and forth in the spacious room.

"But you wanted to," Tarn said, leaning back in his chair. His cerulean hands were folded over his chest, fingers interlaced. To an outsider, he would be the picture of calm, but Kral could see the storm that waged behind his bright indigo eyes.

"Wanting a woman isn't a big deal," Rom said. His tone was even, but his purple eyes blazed with light. Even their "heart-breaker" was being affected by Kral's experience.

Kral didn't want to give them false hope, but he could also give them nothing less than the truth.

"This wasn't simple wanting," Kral said. "While in her presence, I felt a sense of peace such as I've never known. I would have been content to stay there forever. Even...

Even on my own."

Bron sat up straighter and looked over at Kral, his electric blue eyes sparking. Dorn crossed his arms over his massive chest.

"You would leave the prism?" Lar said. He looked stricken.

"That's not what I meant," Kral said. "But when I was with her, I felt complete. Truly complete. As if…"

"As if she's your other half," Nuar said. "Like Lian and I."

That Nuar was certain he'd found his soulmate on Earth was one thing. If Kral's was here as well, the others couldn't deny that Earth was their future—both for themselves and their people.

"A strong reaction," Lar said. "But that doesn't mean she's your mate. She can't be. She isn't Cygnian."

Kral's lips pulled back in a snarl.

Lar raised a hand in a calming gesture. "I only mean that Cygnians and Earthlings aren't biologically compatible."

Rom laughed and raised a shoulder. "Depends on what your definition of that is," he said, with a smirk.

"I'm talking about reproduction." Lar pierced him with a blazing gold glare. "Our souls can't bond with someone that we can't have a family with. If we could, we wouldn't have the population problem our planet is faced with."

The thought pierced Kral's hearts with sadness. The

warriors argued around him, their voices rising.

He wanted a family, but that was beyond him. Beyond all of them. There were too few female Cygnians left.

If Becca wanted children as well, and Kral couldn't give them to her...

The spine plates running down his back stood up, vibrating a warning that matched his frame of mind. The discordant beating of his hearts intensified, as if they wished to reach across his chest and fight each other.

Kral turned and struck the wall. Waves of iridescence rippled out from the spot.

"How am I to know?" he bellowed, silencing everyone. "How am I to know what it will feel like to find the other half of my soul when everything that I am is screaming at me that I've already found it?"

The men remained silent and still. Finally, Nuar stepped forward. He placed his hand on Kral's shoulder and squeezed.

"Let them meet her," Nuar said. "Let them see the bond that the universe has forged between you."

Kral nodded. It was the only way to convince them— until they found soulmates of their own.

Chapter Five

The sub shop was packed. It hadn't been this busy in a while. Becca wished Buddy could see, but he was off doing something with Nika again, leaving his business to Becca to manage.

She could do this. If it would help ease his burden, she would step up.

Becca finished the last of the three sandwiches she was working on and handed them across the counter to the guy standing in front of her. He looked like he was about to say something. That couldn't be good.

He had his food. She had other things to do.

She forced a smile—more baring her teeth than anything—and then purposefully walked to the other end of the bar and started wiping down the counter. The guy seemed to get the message, heading back to his table.

One less thing to worry about.

Becca heard a gasp. She looked over to see a young woman staring at the door with wide eyes.

What now?

Becca turned in time to see three tall, gorgeous men

duck into the shop. And she meant that literally.

They were so tall, they had to bend down a bit to avoid hitting their heads on the lintel. And they had to enter one at a time to make it through the door.

Once inside, they stood in a loose formation, casually surveying the room. Between their stances and just the energy they were putting off, she was pretty sure they were some kind of soldiers. She'd been studying military strategy for as long as she could remember.

Really useful when you ran a sub shop.

The first guy through the door had hair so pale it was almost white. It fell just past his shoulders. His bangs were pulled back from his insanely chiseled face, highlighting strong cheekbones and a jaw that matched his muscular body. His eyes were almost a livid green.

Even though it was sweltering outside, he was wearing weird white leathers and a duster that ended a few inches below his knees. That coat could be hiding a lot of things. Her nerves flared in warning.

The guy flanking him was leaner, but still muscled. His tousled, sandy-brown hair hung about his face, giving him the perfect opportunity to sweep it away from his eyes— which he did—revealing even more gorgeous features. He had a strong, straight nose, a smirk that would gut most women, and a playful spark in his eyes.

His *purple* eyes.

What kind of ren-fair rejects were these?

The man in the center, standing a bit in front of them, had dark brown skin and a mass of thick braids that trailed down his back. He was wearing jeans and a T-shirt, like the purple-eyed man.

All three of them swept their gazes over the shop, taking everything in. When the man with the braids saw Becca behind the counter, his bright yellow gaze fixed on her and held.

She did not like the way he was scowling at her.

Becca was holding her breath. She wasn't sure why, but she couldn't seem to breathe. Her heart was pounding and her mouth went dry. Those freaking tingles were back, racing up and down her spine like someone had connected her upper and lower vertebrae to a battery or something.

The purple-eyed man's face softened into a deep smile, and he kind of half-nodded, half-bowed in her direction. Which was very weird.

Then he stepped aside, letting a fourth man enter the sub shop.

The new guy leaned forward like the others as he entered so he wouldn't hit the doorframe. She recognized the top of his head before he even looked her way.

Bleached strands in rich brown waves. Dark beard and mustache hiding what she was sure was a jaw just as strong as the others', shoulders so broad, he had to angle himself to make it through the door. And those freaky orange eyes that found her immediately, as if she was the only person in the world.

Kral.

The hair on her arms rose as gooseflesh covered her body. Her spine felt electrified, arcs of pleasure spreading out over her back.

Without the chaos of her family and all her worries about Buddy, she didn't have anything to distract her from his presence. And damn, what a presence it was.

He started walking toward her and again it was like the rest of the world disappeared.

Except it hadn't. And someone was talking to her.

She snapped out of...whatever that had been, and turned to the customer standing next to her at the counter.

Three sandwich guy was back. She glanced over to where his friends sat and her heart sank. They were staring at her, leering smiles on their faces. Only one of them seemed to have noticed the group of Viking Warrior wannabes that had just entered the place—the guy who hadn't ordered any food.

"Do you need something?" she asked.

"Your contact number." He cast a cocky smile at her, as if she should feel honored by the request.

On a regular day, the guy wouldn't have pinged her radar. She could tell he was reasonably attractive, if she was into beefy magazine-model dudes with kinda weirdly wide mouths. But she wasn't.

She was into people who were real. Down-to-earth.

And smart and funny and adventurous and playful and caring and...

Yeah, her list was too long. No wonder she hadn't had a date in months.

Looking at this guy—and especially being able to see Kral standing over the guy's shoulder in the background—there was no comparison.

Wait, why was she measuring people against Kral? They'd just met.

She shook herself, and started wiping down the counter. "Not interested," she said.

"Be reasonable," the guy pressed, leaning against the surface right where she was trying to clean. She stopped so that she wouldn't accidentally touch him.

"A female like you—"

Female?

She cut him off. "'Like me?' What exactly does that mean? Because you don't know me at all, so you have no idea what I'm like. Anything you say is bound to be absolutely ignorant."

"I am just trying to invite you to a good time," he said, his charm evaporating.

"I'm fine where I am," she said. The words rang hollow in her mind.

His eyebrows furrowed for a moment, but then he smiled. He leaned forward, rising up on his toes so he could see past the counter. His gaze was comically suggestive when he looked back at her.

"Fine indeed," he said.

Her eyes rolled. She couldn't help it.

"In case you hadn't noticed, my job is to make sandwiches. You have yours, so we're done."

As she moved away, he grabbed her arm, his grip painfully tight. Behind him, she saw Kral arch an eyebrow, but he didn't step in to help.

Odd that it caused more warmth to unfurl in her belly. Not many men would turn down an opportunity to show off their strength.

"Don't be a bi—" the guy holding her arm began.

She was pretty sure she knew where that sentence was going. Too bad for him it was one of her trigger words.

Becca grabbed as much of his short hair as she could and slammed his face into the counter. She managed to angle his head so his nose wouldn't break. Years of practice helped with that—and led to less cleanup.

Broken noses were messy.

The guy staggered back, shaking his head to clear it. Hopefully she'd knocked some manners into him.

"Your food is there." She pointed at the table where his friends sat.

Two of them were glaring at her while the other sat back and smirked. Somehow, the smirking guy set off her warning bells more than the others. She'd never trust a person who came into Buddy's shop and didn't order any food.

"Move along," she said.

"Arrogant female—"

This time, it was Kral's hand coming down on the man's shoulder that kept him from finishing his sentence. She almost wished she'd been able to hear what he was going to say next. This guy was weird.

Kral didn't look mad, though. In fact, he was grinning.

"Greetings," Kral said. "You must be a friend of Becca's."

Her eyebrows shot up her forehead and she felt her mouth drop open.

Friend? *Friend?*

"This female assaulted me," the guy said, jabbing his finger at her. "This food shop is full of witnesses."

Food shop? What the hell?

Becca ground her teeth together to keep from yelling at the guy. She was probably going to have a bruise where he'd grabbed her.

"I told you, you have your food," she said. "We have no further business."

Kral's brows drew together in confusion. His gaze turned to the man, any hint of a smile gone. He spun the guy around and clamped both hands on his shoulders, then bent down to look him in the eye. The three men Kral had entered the bar with came to stand behind him, their sculpted arms crossed over their chests.

"Where I am from, we honor, cherish, and respect all women," Kral said. "If a woman accepts a man's attentions, it is a wondrous event. And if she does not, he learns from the experience and moves on. Reflect on this. Better yourself. Become worthy of winning someone's heart. And someday, if the flow of the universe is kind, it will carry you to the right person."

Kral leaned in closer, sporting a feral smile that was all teeth and no warmth. It kind of reminded Becca of the ones she handed out when she absolutely had to.

"Becca is not that person," Kral said.

Kral spun the guy toward his friends and gave him a push. He staggered forward, barely keeping his footing as he caught himself against the table.

Two of the men who'd been sitting at the table stood. The guy she'd slammed into the counter cast a withering stare at Becca.

Of course, they would blame her for this whole thing. Maybe they'd try a different restaurant next time they were in town. She'd never seen them before and hoped to never see them again.

The fourth man stood, still smirking at her. He didn't match the other three at all in appearance, aside from being tall.

His build was lean and he had short brown hair that stuck up in a carefully disheveled fashion. He was wearing a very nice suit and straightened his tie as he turned his attention to his companions.

His smile became just as predatory as Kral's had been. A shiver went down Becca's spine—and not the pleasant kind she'd been having earlier.

The fourth man didn't say anything, but all three of his companions paled, their skin getting a strange greenish cast. Heads bowed, they turned and exited the diner. The lanky man cast one last smirk at Becca before following them.

"That wasn't creepy at all," Becca murmured under her breath.

Kral and his back-up singers watched the guys leave. As soon as they were gone, Kral and his friends walked over to the counter. All but the pale-haired man sat across from her at the counter. The other guy stood, still surveying the place like some kind of bodyguard.

Most of the people who'd been eating in the shop had stopped to watch the drama unfold. Now, they turned back to their food, whispering in quiet voices.

This probably hadn't been good for the business.

"What the hell was that?" Becca said, throwing her towel over her shoulder. She shouldn't be aiming her anger at Kral, but…what the hell was he even doing here?

"What was what?" Kral asked.

She leaned across the counter, getting in Kral's face, and said, "I had it handled."

"Obviously," Kral said. "It was the man who had no

idea what to do."

The man with the yellow eyes and braids sitting on Kral's right chimed in. "To let him carry on as he was without offering guidance would have been cruel."

The man on Kral's left, with the shoulder-length hair and devastating smile leaned an elbow on the bar. "Some guys just don't know how to treat a lady."

Becca snorted. "I don't see any ladies here."

All three men grinned.

She tried really hard not to care, but deep in her gut, something twisted around in a good way. She wanted to smile back.

She scowled instead.

"Becca, may I present three of my prism," Kral said. "This is Rom and Lar."

He gestured to the blond on his left and then the dark-skinned man on his right in turn. Rom gave her a little salute and Lar inclined his head slightly.

Kral hooked his thumb over his shoulder and, without looking, he said, "That's Dorn."

Dorn grunted.

So that was the guy Kral had quoted at Buddy earlier. Seemed like a real chatterbox.

"Prism, huh?" Becca said. "Is that the name of your basketball team?"

Lar and Rom laughed, but Kral's brow furrowed. He looked confused again.

Lar leaned closer and said, "It's a sport played by two teams who attempt to score points by throwing a ball through a circle while the other team tries to stop them."

"Sounds interesting," Kral said. "Perhaps we should try it."

"Sounds fun." Rom bumped his shoulder against Kral's. Becca had the weirdest surge of envy.

She felt herself leaning toward Kral, shifting her feet so she could be closer to him. And when she did, more of those goosebumps ran up and down her spine. It was like he was putting off some kind of...super-arousing energy field or something.

Damn, she really needed to get out more.

"What are you eating?" Becca said, trying to keep her voice as flat as possible.

Kral opened his hands and gestured in front of him. "Nothing at the moment. Why do you ask?"

"Because I'm the chef," she said. "Or sandwich-maker, anyway. I get people food, and then they get out of my face."

Kral's smile broadened, his white teeth flashing against his light brown skin. "If I don't ask for any food, do I get to stay in your face?"

Any other guy who said that, it would have felt like a line and Becca would have walked away. Something about Kral's tone was oddly sincere, though. Everything about him was sincere. It made her nervous.

Everyone is hiding something.

Buddy and Hayley and Sophie. The people closest to her were pushing her away with their secrets.

Her instincts were screaming at her that this guy in front of her was hiding all kinds of things, no matter how open and honest he seemed.

"If you don't want to eat, what are you and the bod squad doing here?" she asked.

"I'm here for you, of course," Kral said.

Chapter Six

Becca's lips parted as her mouth dropped open. It looked like she was about to say something, but only a choppy breath came out.

Rom elbowed Kral in his ribs. Had he said the wrong thing?

"My prism wanted to meet you," Kral said.

Rom rubbed his hand over his face. Apparently, that wasn't the thing to say to improve the situation.

"What the hell is a prism?" Becca asked.

Her brusque tone sent waves of heat through him. The message it conveyed was clear. She answered to no one and was not afraid to defend herself.

Watching her lash out at the interloper earlier had sent waves of near-electric energy over Kral's skin.

She might not be Cygnian, but she was a warrior.

As Kral began to speak, Rom quickly said, "Friends. It means we're friends."

"Closer than friends," Kral corrected, putting an arm around Lar and Rom's shoulders. "We are lifemates, all of us."

Becca arched an eyebrow. "And there's more than the four of you involved in that?"

"Seven, in total." Kral sat up straighter. "A full spectrum."

Her eyebrows kept creeping up her forehead and her cheeks pinked. "Damn. That'd be something to see."

"*Platonic* lifemates," Rom said.

"Oh." Becca glanced between them, only her eyes moving. "Okay. I'm still waiting for you to explain why you wanted to meet me."

"We heard your song," Rom said.

Becca shook her head. "Again with the song. It was just some four-part harmony. We're not even that good."

"You underestimate yourself," the guy with the yellow eyes said. Lar. Right. He paused for a few moments, undoubtedly considering his next words with care. "We are very good at analyzing frequencies and vibrations. Your family has extraordinary skill in merging your voices to great effect."

"Probably because our mom has made us practice every year of our lives just for our special Christmas family musical," Becca said.

"Then we owe her a debt," Lar said. "Hearing your song was truly a gift."

Becca snorted, then started wiping the counter again. "So, what? You're agents who want to sign me or something?"

"We aren't agents," Kral said. "We are warriors."

Becca's eyebrows lifted again. Then she laughed.

She laughed at his proclamation of being a warrior.

Did she need to see evidence? Because he could track down the man she had…dispatched herself earlier.

All right, that man was dealt with, but Kral could find someone else to challenge. He would show her his prowess, his worth as—

As what? A mate?

As Lar and Rom continued conversing with Becca, Kral sank back onto his stool, realizing how foolish this trip truly was.

Becca wasn't Cygnian. They could never be mates. Perhaps if Kral belonged to a different house, it would be different. But he wasn't.

He was the crown prince.

He owed it to his people to find a suitable mate, even though there were so few females left on his homeworld. Their scientists had been working for generations to try to bring back balance, but every year higher doses of radiation from the nearby black hole had been leaking into their planet's atmosphere through the crystal sphere protecting it, somehow resulting in a surge in male offspring.

Even if his people would accept an otherworlder into the royal family, Becca would have to prove her worth. She would have to challenge him to battle—and win.

If Kral challenged her, his people would know he could easily defeat her. They wouldn't accept the victory.

Kral had seen Becca's fire. He had watched her defend herself against that man earlier. But she wouldn't stand a chance against a Cygnian warrior.

In the end, she was only human.

"Hang on," Becca said, moving away from them.

Watching her walk away tugged at his hearts. He began to stand, but then forced himself to sit back down.

She started talking to another human who had entered the shop. After a moment, she exchanged currency with them, then headed through a doorway into another room. Kral could watch her work through an open window between the spaces.

Rom turned to Kral, smiling. "I like her," Rom said.

"I knew you would." Kral shook his head. "Not that it makes any difference."

Rom's brow furrowed. "What do you mean?"

"She can't be my soulmate," Kral said.

"Has your reaction to her changed?" Rom asked.

"If anything, it's stronger." Kral shook his head. "It makes no sense for me to feel this… This pull."

Lar was silent for several moments. His lips were pinched tight and his hands fisted.

"What is it?" Kral asked.

Lar shook his head sharply, then let out a long breath. "Something is there. I can feel it."

"You can?" A thrum of surprise swept through Kral.

"I believe I can," Lar said. "We two were the first members of this prism. Our connection is strong."

"You've been telling Nuar that his bond with Lian can't be a soulmate bond," Kral said. "You said they can only form among Cygnians."

Lar looked thoughtful, then turned to face Kral. "The day we met, we saved each other's lives. I swore an oath to you, pledging my life to yours until the day I die. I would be breaking that oath if I didn't tell you that... perhaps I was wrong."

Kral looked back to Becca. She glanced at him as she was handing some sandwiches to her latest customer and froze as their gazes locked.

Something passed between them. Something strong enough to make Kral's breath catch in his chest.

And he was certain she felt it, too.

The person she was talking to rapped their hand on the counter a few times. Becca started, then turned and said something that made the other person pale and back away a few steps. They hastily grabbed their sandwiches and fled.

She was fierce. But was she his?

"We need to be certain," Kral said.

"I agree." Lar was silent for a few moments, then asked, "Have you spoken to your parents about this?"

"No. I wasn't sure what to say and didn't want to

sound…"

"Desperate?" Rom suggested.

Kral scoffed. "I suppose that's one word for it."

"If it's true that we can find our mates on Earth, though, this would be a wonderful thing for our people," Rom said. "With the Vegans here, we might even be able to find a way to have children with them."

"Would our people truly welcome those offspring, though?" Kral asked. "They wouldn't be purely Cygnian."

"Is your sister Sorca any less Cygnian than we, due to her Sadirian DNA?" Lar said.

The vertebrae along Kral's spine shifted, the spine plates that normally lay flat against his back trying to stand up and pressing against the thin fabric of his shirt. His lips peeled back from his teeth in a snarl.

"Sorca is as much a Cygnian as we are, no matter that her genetics were manipulated by those cowards in the Coalition," Kral said.

"There is your answer," Lar said. "But calm yourself before you poke holes in that flimsy shirt."

Kral took a few deep breaths, pushing away the anger he always felt when thinking of his sister's mistreatment at the hands of Coalition scientists. He felt his spine plates settle back down.

"There is a connection," Kral said.

Rom nodded. "And a strong one, if Lar can feel it, too."

"We should return to the ship and see if your parents can offer any insight into this." Lar stood and nodded to Dorn.

"Agreed." Kral drew himself up from his stool.

Becca noticed them rise. She said something to the person she'd been talking to, then walked along the length of the counter toward them. Though her gait was casual, he thought he saw some tension around her eyes. Could it mean she wanted him to stay?

"Heading out?" she said, brusquely. She planted her palms on the counter's surface and leaned forward, eyeing the men before her.

"We have an important matter to attend to," Lar said.

"But I will return," Kral added.

"You better," she said.

For a moment, Kral's hearts seemed to stop, then suddenly they pounded against the sides of his chest.

Until she continued.

"Buddy isn't talking to me, and that's not right." She nodded at Kral. "I'm not going to push him anymore, but when you come back, I want you to bring me some answers."

He smiled, baring his teeth. "That is precisely what I intend to do."

Kral turned and followed his prism from the bar. He could feel Becca's gaze on him until the door shut behind him.

"She has spirit," Lar said.

Dorn surveyed the parking lot. "She has strength."

"And she has intelligence." Rom clasped Kral's shoulder. "She is a worthy mate."

"She also has questions that her brother would rather she not have answers to," Kral said.

"Are you going to let him make that decision for her?" Lar asked.

Kral laughed. "Of course not."

They walked from the building, heading toward their cloaked ship. At first, they passed several Earthlings at a time, walking along the same streets and sidewalks. As the buildings fell into greater disrepair, the people became more sparse, until there was only the four of them.

They turned and began to cross a large field between two derelict buildings, sand shifting beneath their feet with each step. Rom quickened his stride.

"What the hell is it with this planet?" he said. "Everything's soft. Even the ground."

"The footing is more solid in Harbor," Lar said. "But this place has its appeal."

"This place has Becca," Rom said. "That's the appeal."

They passed through the perimeter of their ship's cloaking field, revealing the beautiful crystalline ship floating above the ground. The bottom hatch slid open, bathing the ground beneath it in light.

Lar turned to Rom and said, "I've been meaning to ask,

what did you tell Vay about us taking our ship out of the hangar?"

"I told her we had a mission." Rom shrugged. "She was too polite to ask about it."

It didn't sit well with Kral that they were misleading their contact at Harbor, even if she was a Coalition soldier. She had treated them well and acted honorably, as far as Kral could tell.

Then again, the Coalition had tricked them before.

They stepped into the circle of light beneath their ship, then leapt the twenty feet into the belly of their vessel. Once inside, Dorn sealed the hatch.

"Lar, connect the holodisplay with my parents' secured communications relay," Kral said.

Lar nodded, then led the way to the common room. They hadn't been there long before Tarn, Bron, and Nuar showed up, taking positions around the room.

"What did you find?" Tarn asked, ever inquisitive.

"We aren't sure," Lar said.

Lar might not be sure, but Kral was becoming moreso with each moment. He just wasn't sure what to do about it. He stood in the center of the common room, hoping his parents would have some answers.

Several crystal formations near the ceiling rippled with a full spectrum of colors before beaming an image of his father's office into one side of the common room. An empty chair grown of sapphire sat behind his smoky quartz desk, the hologram so complete, Kral almost felt as if he was back on Cygnus-Prime.

His father appeared abruptly as he stepped into the space being recreated on the *Arrow*. Still tying his robe, the king sat down and leaned on the large quartz desk. His hair stood out from his scalp at odd angles, and he was smoothing a hand over his light-blue beard.

"Do you know what time it is on Cygnus-Prime?" he asked.

"Apologies, father, but the matter is urgent," Kral said.

His father's expression grew somber and he straightened in his chair. "Another attack by the Tau Centauran Assembly?"

"No." Kral looked at the men standing around him, saw the hope flicker in their eyes. He turned back to his father and said, "I believe I've found my soulmate. Here on Earth."

His father's gaze intensified, his expression more serious than if Kral had spoken of an attack. He looked aside, his hand curling into a fist on the table.

Kral had expected his father to laugh and ask if Kral was joking. Or perhaps to tell him he was seeing what he wanted to see.

Instead, he said, "Are you sure?"

He wouldn't meet Kral's gaze.

"I am," Kral said. "Why do you not seem surprised?"

Finally, his father looked at him. "Is she Sadirian?"

"Sadirian?" Kral took a step back, repulsed at the idea. "No, she's from Earth."

"An Earthling?" Now, his father did laugh, and it incensed Kral. "No, that will never work. Earth is too technologically and socially stunted to produce a viable mate for you."

Lar came to stand at Kral's side. "If she is Kral's soulmate, we can't ignore that bond."

"Kral's mate will eventually be queen," Father said, voicing Kral's own concerns. "If she's an Earthling, she has no understanding of our ways. How could she hope to earn the right to stand at his side by defeating him in combat of any kind? Our people could perhaps accept a mate challenge from a Sadirian soldier, genetically engineered for battle, but not a primitive—"

"Father," Kral roared. The walls of the chamber echoed with the sound, the floor beneath him vibrating from it.

His father's brow furrowed and a muscle in his cheek tightened enough that Kral could clearly see it through his beard. No other Cygnian would dare speak to the king that way.

"Becca is not primitive," Kral said. "Nor are her people."

"Becca." His father canted his head to the side. "Why do I know that name?"

"She's one of Buddy's sisters," Lar said.

"Buddy?" Father nodded. "That makes sense, then.

Earthlings are nearly identical to Sadirians genetically. You feel a bond toward Buddy. Of course you feel connected to his family."

"That isn't what this is," Kral said. Only his prism knew the truth of why Kral had invited Buddy into their trust—of why Kral had been trying to ally the Cygnians with Earth.

It was because of Becca. The way her voice had stirred Kral's soul, made his hearts beat almost in unity. If the stories he had heard were true, he was certain she was his soulmate.

"It's good that there is a link." His father went on as if he hadn't heard Kral speak. "This is an auspicious beginning."

"To what?" Kral demanded.

His father was silent for a few moments. His gaze swept the room—recreated in his own office back on Cygnus-Prime in the same detail—lingering on each of the men in Kral's prism, before returning to his son.

"To a second chance for our people," he said. "A chance at a future."

"The Cygnians have always had a future." Kral struck his chest. "We are the most fearsome warriors in the galaxy."

"Yes, we go into battle and we come out unscathed." His father's tone was laced with bitterness. "And what do we return to? A planet bereft of daughters. An enemy not even we can stand against."

"What enemy is that?" Lar asked.

His father's lips pulled up in a snarl. *"Time.* Do you know how many female children were born to us in the last fifteen cycles?"

Kral opened his mouth to speak, but his father continued first.

"None," he said. "Not a single daughter has graced our planet."

"Cygnians don't reproduce quickly," Kral said, reaching for a way to explain that didn't make the plates on his spine long to stand on end. "It could simply be an anomaly."

"It's not an anomaly and you know it." His father's gaze raked everyone in the room. "You all know it. Every year, the imbalance worsens."

"What can we do?" Rom asked.

"Our plan is already in motion," his father said.

Misgiving crept along Kral's spine.

"Father, what have you done?" Kral asked.

Father looked Kral in the eye, and said, "What we had to."

Nuar stepped closer to the image of the king. "Sorca... We thought the High Council was lying when they said there was a treaty—that you had *given* them Cygnian DNA."

The misgiving turned to electric dread, shooting

through Kral's nerves. His stomach churned up acid into the back of his throat.

"You wouldn't have," Kral said. "You couldn't have known what they were going to do with it."

Father's voice was as cold as the crystal desk he leaned on. "They were supposed to find a way to make our species compatible."

Kral's spine plates flared. He sucked in a breath through his nose, the muscles in his arms bunching. His claws extended, every atom in his body screamed at him to fight…something *anything*. What he was hearing couldn't be true.

Half his prism had crouched as he was, lips peeled back and bodies ready for battle. The air around them vibrated as their spine plates shivered in warning.

Only Lar, Dorn, and Rom still stood straight. Dorn's eyes had flared a brilliant green, and he held so still, Kral wasn't sure he was even breathing.

Lar came up to stand behind Kral, resting a hand on his shoulder. "Let our king explain."

Kral waited, knowing that any explanation wouldn't be good enough to justify what Sorca had been through.

"One offspring," his father said. "One. That was our agreement. A way to prove that their genetic therapies could make them capable of carrying Cygnian children to term. We had no idea they would twist our words and abuse our trust as they did."

"Wait, you expected Sadirian women to give birth to Cygnians?" Rom said. "They won't even give birth to other Sadirians."

Tarn jumped in as soon as Rom paused. "Sadirians don't have children. They grow whatever kind of sentients they want in vats until they're adults, then program their minds with whatever trash their government wants them to think is true."

"The survival of our species is at stake," his father bellowed. "We will adapt. In time, we may find ways to have children naturally. There are quadrillions of Sadirians in the galaxy. You will find your soulmates among them. Proper partners."

"Proper?" Kral nearly choked on the word.

"Think of your prism, Kral," Father said. "Your souls are all linked. If you claim your mate on Earth, you're constraining them to the same fate. They will only be able to find mates on that one small planet, filled with only a few billion sentients—who fervently believe they're the only intelligent life in existence."

Nuar stepped forward forcefully. "Earthlings are more adaptable than you know. I have found my soulmate here. She is strong and fierce. And we have achieved frequency. I've seen the prismatic effect of our union."

"You saw what you wanted to see," Father yelled. "Now that we know the project was a success, we can access the Coalition's genetic database and find likely matches for you all. Your entire generation will be spared from never finding your soulmate."

"Wait..." Lar shook his head. "This was the plan all along? Ally yourself with the Coalition as long as it meant we could breed with them?"

"It's worse than that," Nuar said. "He mentioned genetic therapies. We would have to alter ourselves to become compatible. And at that point, would we even be Cygnian anymore?"

"My sister is a Cygnian," Kral said. "No matter how much Sadirian DNA has been spliced into her."

"We can't let this—" Tarn began.

"It's done." Dorn's steady voice cut him off. He stood with his arms crossed, his distant gaze looking at the king and yet through him. He spoke so rarely, every warrior in the room stopped to give him their full attention.

"Sorca has been active for dozens of cycles," Dorn said. "And our king is speaking as if we are all already compatible with others, even if our children will need to be crafted in a laboratory."

Kral had been so upset, he hadn't thought through all the ramifications of his father's words. But Dorn was right.

"We've been altered," Nuar said.

"Half our population volunteered for the procedure," Father said. "Including Ehmach and I. Every participant was ordered not to tell their offspring, in case it didn't work. We didn't want to get your hopes up. The only change to your DNA is that you are compatible with Sadirians."

"And Earthlings," Kral said.

"Just because their genetics are similar does not mean they're compatible," Father said. "We know that Sadirians are, even though our scientists will need to be involved to create children. Regardless, Earth is not a site for potential soulmates."

"It is," Kral insisted. "I've felt the bond."

"How would you even know?" Father said. "This could be just a glimmer of what true frequency can be. If you try to bond yourself to her, you'll be denying yourself the chance to find your true mate—and denying every warrior in your prism the same. Can you live with that?"

Kral stood straighter. "I can."

Because he knew his father was wrong.

Father sighed again. "I can't. Kral, I forbid you from seeing this Earthling again. You are to return to Cygnus-Prime so that we can create a plan for forming an alliance with the Coalition of Planets in exchange for the genetic information we will need to find soulmate bonds for our people."

"Father—"

"I have spoken," he said. "You are the crown prince. Someday, you'll be king. Stop thinking of yourself and think of your people."

The hologram flickered, then vanished. For a time, all Kral heard was the discordant beating of his hearts in his ears, his heavy breaths as he tried to calm himself.

Was he being selfish? Finding one's soulmate was revered in their culture. His father shouldn't be throwing the possibility aside so quickly.

And yet...

Kral didn't even know if Becca would accept him, once she knew who—and what—he truly was.

"Your father is wrong." Rom broke the silence. "I saw you together. Even I felt an echo of your bond. And if your soulmate is here on Earth, then ours are, too."

"We don't follow where you go because you're our prince," Tarn said. "But because our souls all vibrate in harmony. It's been that way since each of us met and will continue to be that way until each of us returns to the stones. If you've found your mate here, so will we."

Kral wanted to believe them. But in his hearts, he wondered if perhaps his father was right.

There was only one way to be sure. He had to return to Becca, to spend more time with her. He had to know.

"In that case," Kral said, "it's time to defy the king."

Chapter Seven

Becca's feet hurt and her back was stiff. Nothing new after a long shift. It didn't usually bother her, but her mood had soured after Kral and his *prism* left.

Especially since he didn't come back.

She kicked a stone out of her way as she walked down the sidewalk near her house. She should be home resting up for tomorrow, but that restlessness was worse than ever, her spine a constant line of tingles. Walking usually cleared her head.

Not tonight.

A dog barked somewhere far off and she could hear the drone of cars on the distant highway, even this late. She wondered absently if one of those cars belonged to Kral and he was keeping his word and coming back to her.

Why did she care? He was just some guy.

No he isn't.

Okay, he was Buddy's friend. And he was gorgeous. And he obviously cared deeply about others.

And he knew Buddy's secrets.

That should have irked her, since she was used to being

Buddy's confidant. Instead, knowing that Kral was out there supporting her brother made her feel better.

With such a big family, Becca knew a lot of parents would have looked to the eldest daughter to take on more of the tasks of raising her younger siblings and helping out with the cousins. Becca was the eldest girl.

But Buddy had stepped into the role like he was born for it. Their parents were great, but they had both needed jobs to keep the family afloat. Buddy had cooked for his sisters, mended their clothes, tended their bruises, and chased off their bullies—until Becca and Sophie finally managed to convince him that they could fight for themselves.

Then he'd taught them to fight. Practiced with them till he felt okay taking more of a backseat. She knew he still watched over them, though. And she'd always have his back.

Now, *Kral* was watching Buddy's back. Becca had to admit, he was a hell of a lot more intimidating than she could ever be.

That must be why she was upset. She didn't want to be replaced. It had to be the reason.

That's not the reason.

"Agh, shut up!" she said, going out of her way to kick another pebble into the street. "He's just some dumb guy, and guys are trouble. They tie you up in knots inside and mess up your life and…"

And leave.

They always left, for one reason or another.

"It wasn't working out." "It wasn't her, it was them."

But if it really wasn't her, why did they always end up dumping her?

Her family was her top priority. She knew that had run off a few guys she'd dated. They actually said they didn't think they'd ever be as important to her as her family.

She couldn't argue the point. None of the guys she'd dated had really gotten under her skin.

It was bullshit that they thought Becca couldn't make room in her heart for people not born into her family. Hayley had started out as a friend. Now, Becca was as close to her as to her sisters. Those guys just hadn't had the guts to stick it out and earn a place in Becca's heart.

Becca knew she could be abrasive. She didn't back down from a fight. She spoke her mind, and if people didn't like it, they could take a hike.

Which they did.

Yeah, it probably *was* her. But she wasn't going to change for anyone. She just needed to find someone who could accept her for herself.

She scratched at her back, the line of tingles on her spine intensifying. If this kept up, she was going to have to visit a neurologist. Like she could afford that.

It was probably just the humidity. The tingles spread over her back, then traveled down her arms and legs.

"What the hell?" she murmured.

Something crunched on the sidewalk behind her. A footstep.

Who the hell would be out walking this late? Besides her, anyway.

She didn't let her steps falter, pretending she hadn't heard anything.

"Oh, damn," she said, shaking her head.

She pulled her purse around in front of her body, shielding it from view from anyone behind her. She hoped the person thought she had just forgotten something.

Forgot to have my pepper spray ready.

She pulled out the small cartridge that Buddy had given them all as late Christmas presents. He'd missed the actual holiday because he was helping with Nika on some sort of secret emergency. Apparently, one that involved Kral.

Becca flicked off the safety. The footsteps were closer now, an occasional crunch as sand and grit caught beneath the guy's shoes.

She was sure it was a guy. The clomping steps almost sounded like he was wearing boots—in Florida during the summer? She could also tell he was only a few steps away and closing fast.

Someone grabbed her shoulder.

How was his reach so long?

She whipped her arm up as she turned, spraying the pepper spray…at his chest. She had seriously misjudged his height.

And she actually wasn't spraying his chest.

The moment she turned, the guy ducked to the side faster than she'd ever seen anyone move. He grabbed her wrist and yanked her aim off even farther, so the spray dissipated in the air harmlessly.

She kicked the side of his knee to take him down. Pain lanced up her foot and calf when she connected. It felt like kicking a fire hydrant.

What the hell?

She went for his eyes with her free hand, pointing her fingers so she could blind him. Except...

His eyes were glowing. They were glowing *orange*.

Kral?

Again, with the lightning reflexes, Kral grabbed her other wrist and held her, his grip firm and inescapable.

He smiled, leaning down so their faces were close. His teeth looked a little sharper than they should have been.

She swallowed hard.

"I think perhaps I should have let you know I was behind you sooner," he said.

"You think?"

Her breath was still coming fast, her heart pounding against her ribs.

He'd given her a scare. She'd calm down any second now. Any second.

Except heat was spilling through her veins where he

touched her, flooding her body and making her core molten with need. Her fingers twitched with the urge to run them through that wild mane of hair. Or better yet, to pull his tight T-shirt over his head and explore the lines of muscle she could clearly see beneath the fabric.

"You are fierce," he rumbled, stepping a bit closer.

There wasn't that much space between them in the first place. She could feel the heat he was putting off.

Goosebumps ran along the skin of her exposed arms. Her body was just a mass of tingling pleasure at this point.

"Yeah… Well… Thanks." Dammit, why did her voice sound so breathless?

Maybe because he's taking your breath away?

She wanted to groan at the cheesy thought.

This wasn't her. Nobody had this effect on her.

Nobody made her knees weak or her breath catch in her throat. Nobody's touch sent shockwaves through her body and lit her up like a lightning storm. Nobody made her want to plaster herself to them and wrap her arms around their neck and hold on tight and never let go.

"What are you…" Her mouth had gone dry and she had to swallow to continue. "What are you doing here?"

"I needed to see you again."

"Oh. Is Buddy okay?"

"Your brother is fine. I appreciate your concern for him." Kral's smile deepened. "If I release you, will you attack me again?"

Something about his tone made it almost sound like a request.

"Depends," she said.

His eyes widened. The light from the street lamps was still doing something weird and making them look like they were glowing. Or maybe they were glow-in-the-dark contacts?

That was ridiculous. There was definitely something going on with that color, though.

He tugged on her wrists, pulling her closer to him. Her arms were pressed against his chest. She craned her neck back, unable to break away from his gaze.

He leaned down and she thought maybe he was going to kiss her.

Please, please, please, kiss me.

What the hell was wrong with her? This wasn't... This couldn't...

"Depends on what?" he asked, his warm breath brushing over her face.

"Are you going to surprise me again?"

He grinned, flashing those extra-sharp teeth at her once more. "Undoubtedly."

From anyone else, she would have thought of that as a presumptuous line. From Kral, it sent more goosebumps racing over her.

There was a promise in that word. One that had her mind spinning.

How was he going to surprise her? When? Would it involve more touching? Certain skill sets that she hadn't had a chance to explore in way too long?

Kral pressed her hands against his chest, holding them there with one massive palm. He used his free hand to push her hair behind her ear.

Except that wasn't really what he did. A normal guy might have, but Kral took his huge, strong hand and ran all of his fingers through her hair, dragging his nails lightly across her scalp as he did.

More lighting. More fire heating her core.

Her eyes fluttered shut and she leaned into his touch.

"Becca," he said, his voice very, very close.

"Yeah."

She forced her eyes open, wanting to see this. Wanting to know if he was feeling the same kind of amazing pull as she was.

His eyes were glowing like twin stars.

So beautiful. Impossibly beautiful. Impossible.

All of this was impossible. And yet, she could feel the hard muscles of his chest beneath her hands, the strong beat of—

Wait… She could feel a pounding in his chest, but it wasn't coming from the center. She slid her hands across his pecs, toward the sides of his body. The beats grew stronger. *Beats.*

"Becca." He said her name again, angling his head and

shifting closer in a way that left no doubt whatsoever that he was about to kiss her.

And she wanted him to. She wanted to kiss him. More than she'd ever wanted to kiss anyone in her life.

Even though she'd just met him.

Even though she barely knew anything about him.

Even though...

He has two hearts. There are two hearts beating against his ribs and they are not at all where they're supposed to be.

Glowing orange eyes. Sharp teeth. A body as hard as stone, putting off some kind of aura that had her melting in a puddle at his feet.

And she didn't even care.

Maybe she hadn't gone for a walk. She could have fallen asleep back at home and was having some kind of weird, erotic dream.

If so, she didn't want to wake up.

When his lips were a whisper away from hers, he said, "May I?"

"If you don't, I'm going to kick your ass again."

Another smile. He had a great smile, sharp teeth and all. And great lips that he needed to—

Kral's brow furrowed and he suddenly straightened. He pulled Becca against his side, breaking the spell of the moment.

What had she been about to do? And...dream or no

dream, could they maybe get back to that?

The sound of scrabbling claws and panting breaths drew her attention back to reality. A border collie came rushing up to them, barking frantically.

"Dash?" Becca said.

Kral relaxed a bit beside her, enough that she could break away from his grasp. "Sophie's dog."

"Yeah." Becca approached the agitated animal, dropping to one knee. "It's okay, girl. Come on. It's me."

Dash ran toward her a few paces, then dropped her forelegs to the ground. She kept her butt up in the air, but her tail wasn't wagging. She jumped back several feet and started spinning in circles.

"You don't have to show off your agility moves for me," Becca said. "But how the hell did you get out of the house? Does Sophie know you're gone?"

Dash stopped spinning, but then started barking again. At this rate, the neighbors would be calling the cops on them.

"Hey, settle down, girl," Becca said. "Come on. Come here."

Dash whimpered, her nose close to the ground as she approached. As soon as she was in reach, Becca grabbed her collar and tugged the dog against her chest.

Dash was trembling all over. A feeling of misgiving threaded through Becca, chasing away the last vestiges of the much more pleasant feelings Kral had evoked.

"What happened?" Becca petted Dash, trying to get her to calm down.

Something sticky and viscous was smeared around her mouth and down her chest.

"What is this all over you?" Becca pulled one hand away from the dog's scruff. It was coated in a vibrant green liquid.

"It's blood." Kral stepped closer to her, his gaze scanning their surroundings.

"It's *green*."

"I didn't say it was human blood."

Chapter Eight

Becca snorted. She turned back to Dash and used a cloying voice to say, "Have you been biting Vulcans?"

The dog had undoubtedly been biting something. Kral had one highly unsettling idea of what it had been. Before forming his own conclusion, he needed to know what Becca was talking about.

"What are Vulcans?" Kral asked, maintaining his vigil on their surroundings.

"Aliens from the planet Vulcan," she said. "You know, like Mr. Spock?"

His hearts seemed to pause, then began a frantic, arrhythmic beat. He turned his full attention to her.

She already knew that aliens were real? Why had Buddy been so intent on keeping his family away from Kral and his prism then? Becca didn't seem bothered by aliens at all.

Kral had never heard of Vulcan before. Perhaps Cygnians had a different name for the planet.

"Is he hostile?" Kral asked.

"Who?"

"Mr. Spock."

Becca smirked. "Well, he can be. Just don't piss him off. He's stronger than humans and even though he doesn't seem to have emotions, he does. He just hides them well."

Interesting. There were several alien species she could be speaking of. But none of them had green blood.

"We should check on your sisters," Kral said.

"Yeah. Sophie would be worried sick if she knew Dash was running around out here. I need a leash for her."

Kral pulled his shirt from his jeans, then grabbed the hem and tore a few inches from the bottom of the ridiculously frail fabric. Luckily, it was long enough that his spine plates would still be covered. His holo-emitter could change the color of his skin and hair, but not his physiology.

When he had a strip a few feet long, he offered it to Becca. She ignored it, her wide eyes focused on his stomach.

He felt his chest expand with a huge breath and tightened his muscles. From the way she'd reacted to him earlier, she no doubt saw him as a potential lover. But he wanted her to see him as a mate. She needed to know he was strong enough to protect her, to care for her, and give her everything she needed.

Her brow furrowed and she canted her head to the side. "That's...a lot of abs."

Kral lifted his shirt and looked down. Five rows of

abdominal muscles corded his stomach. Was that more or less than humans had?

Becca had seemed surprised, but she made a little choking sound when he lifted his shirt. Her eyes widened as she looked up at the rest of what he'd exposed, her gaze heating again.

The dog barked.

He dropped the hem of his shirt and knelt next to Dash. Buddy had brought Pickles along on several of their adventures and often put a leash on the animal to keep him from running off. Kral quickly tied the fabric to Dash's collar, then stood, keeping a firm grip on it.

"Let's go," he said.

Becca nodded and rose beside him. He set the quickest pace that she could keep up with, bearing in mind that his strides were three times the length of hers.

"Does Buddy know?" Kral asked.

"Know what? What's there to know?" Her cheeks turned bright red.

"About you and Mr. Spock. That you're aware of his existence."

She snorted. "Yeah, we used to hang out together and watch TV all the time when we were kids."

They hung out with aliens? But Buddy had acted as if he'd never seen an alien before. It didn't make sense.

If Becca already knew about aliens—and accepted them—it would be that much easier for her to accept Kral.

Hope swelled in his hearts.

"You look surprised," she said. "Are you one of those guys who thinks that girls can't be into sci-fi?"

"Sci-fi?" He'd heard that word before.

"Science fiction. You know, aliens and spaceships and ray guns. I used to watch B sci-fi movies with my parents all the time. We still watch them together sometimes. Buddy wasn't quite as into it, but Hayley would join in and bring Sophie along."

Kral's hopes crashed around him in fiery wreckage. She was talking about television shows. Entertainment.

"So, Mr. Spock is a character in one of those movies," Kral said, his tone subdued.

"A couple. We mostly watched him on TV. All Amy wants to watch are crime procedurals. No imagination on that kid." Becca stopped in front of a dwelling with two levels to it, judging by the windows. "This is our place."

The yard was scrubby, like most in this area. Bits of grass clung to the sand and a small tree stood in the center of the space. Large orange spheres covered it.

Dash tugged on the strip of fabric and started barking again.

"Quiet, Dash," Becca said. "You'll wake the neighbors."

"Take the leash."

Kral handed over the fabric, then stood facing the house. He couldn't focus on his own disappointment right now.

The blood on Dash might not belong to Mr. Spock the Vulcan, but Kral had a good idea of where it had come from. There was another species of sentients with green blood that was at the top of Kral's list of possibilities.

The Tau Ceti.

Kral struck his wristbands together, then hummed the note to activate his scanners.

"What the hell was that?" Becca said. "You be quiet, too!"

She turned from him and headed toward the door. Kral followed after, reading the small holo-display projecting from his right wrist.

No active energy signatures. No signs of traps or hazards. One humanoid life sign. A human female, unconscious. Kral hoped she was just sleeping.

Becca placed her key in the lock of the front door and turned it, then paused. "That's weird. It's already unlocked."

She cautiously pushed the door open. Dash darted through the small space.

"Dash," she hissed. "Aw, come on. Why do you only listen to Sophie?"

Kral didn't try to stop her when she flipped on the lights. Perhaps he should have.

Becca froze at the scene before them.

They stood at the entrance to a living room. What had

once been a long, low table lay in splinters. Several cushions were missing from the couch, strewn about the room. A large bookshelf that ran the length of the floor to the ceiling had been overturned, its contents splayed over the floor.

The room was muggy, the evening's warmth and humidity entering through a large opening in the wall that probably once housed one of the sliding partitions made of glass that Earthlings used to "secure" their dwellings. The glass had been vaporized, his scans showing only molecular traces of the material.

"What the hell happened here?" Becca slowly walked deeper into the room, dropping Dash's lead. The dog darted through the debris.

"Sophie?" Becca yelled. "Amy?"

Dash began to bark, nosing at something on the ground under the bookcase. Becca ran over, Kral right behind her.

"Oh my God." She pulled away some cushions as Kral lifted the bookshelf and tossed it away.

Amy was lying very still on the floor.

Not just sleeping.

A gash ran down her forehead and her clothing was burned near her collarbone. Her shirt looked as though it had partially melted into the scorched skin beneath it.

"Amy? Amy!" Becca dropped to her knees. Dash was right at her side.

The fabric they'd used as a lead was still tied to the

dog's collar. Becca quickly untied it, then wadded it up and pressed it against the cut on Amy's forehead.

Becca turned to Kral and said, "Call an ambulance. We need to... To stabilize her neck. We can't move her. Jesus, what could have done this to her?"

The scanner in Kral's wristband was still set on a broad scan. He hummed a deep note, far below what Becca could hear, that would send a distress call to his prism. Then he shifted notes, activating the biometric medical scanning function.

Becca put her hand on Amy's chest. "She's breathing. Okay, that's good. But... Why are you just standing there?"

"I'm waiting for you to move aside," Kral said.

"What?"

He kicked more debris away, clearing a space, then knelt next to the sisters. Keeping his hand a few inches above Amy's body, he let it slowly drift over the obvious wounds before scanning the rest of her.

"What are you doing? I asked you to call for help." Becca bit out each word. "Never mind, I'll do it myself."

She started digging through her purse with her free hand, her gaze flicking back to where she was also carefully applying pressure to Amy's wound. Kral grabbed Becca's wrist, noting the current that passed between them even during this.

"Help is on the way," he said.

"You called an ambulance?" She looked around, as if evidence of that act would be lying on the floor somewhere. "When? How?"

"Not an ambulance."

"Then who did you call?" she asked.

"My prism."

"Your... What?"

"The men who serve with me," he said.

"Serve... Like military? Are you with the military? How does that help my sister?"

Kral spread his fingers, increasing the light on the visual display on his wristband to a brightness that Becca could see as well. She gasped as a small holographic projection of her sister's body floated above Kral's forearm. He tapped the transparent projection of Amy's head in the display, momentarily disrupting the pale blue light it consisted of.

A close-up of just her cranium spiraled before them. White light highlighted areas around the gash on her forehead.

The image zoomed in again, showing Amy's brain. Gold readouts let Kral know there was no damage there, thankfully.

"Okay, if that's what it looks like, it's really helpful," Becca said. "How does that even work? It's—"

Her words cut off with a sharp inhalation as the scan revealed more about Amy's injuries. Blinking white lights surrounded scorched tissue and damaged organs.

The blast had to have come from close. Why hadn't her attacker vaporized her?

Kral's spine plates stiffened as he thought of Sophie. Becca had expected both of her sisters to be home.

His scan of the house revealed that Amy was the only person within. She was the one he could help right now.

He opened vocal communications with the *Arrow* and said, "Nuar, have you received this data?"

"Yes," Nuar said. "Don't move her. She has injuries to several vital organs from some form of blunt-force trauma."

Becca looked around, as if trying to find the source of the voice.

"A large bookshelf fell on her," Kral said.

"That would explain the bruising patterns." Nuar's tone was somber. "We're two minutes out."

They must be pushing the *Arrow* to its limits for atmospheric travel to arrive so quickly.

"See you soon, then." Kral ended the transmission.

"Who was that?" Becca said. "Was that the help you called for?"

"That was Nuar. He's my chief medical officer. And yes, he can help. It won't be long."

Becca nodded, then turned her attention back to her sister. Amy's eyelids fluttered.

"Sophie," she managed.

"Oh my God... Sophie." Becca looked around, as if she might find her other sister amidst the debris. "It's okay, Amy. It's okay. We'll find her."

Becca looked around with a pained expression before turning her gaze back to the injury on Amy's head. Finally, she looked to Kral.

"Can you find her?" Becca said. "I can't leave Amy, but if Sophie is here..."

Kral reached out and rested his hand on Becca's back. "She isn't. I scanned the house before we entered."

"Scanned it? How."

He lifted his arm and showed her his wristband.

"What are those things?" she asked. "How do they work?"

"Becca—"

Before he could say more, Dash perked up, her ears standing straight on her head. She ran toward the opening in the wall that led to the back yard and started barking incessantly.

"What is it now?" Becca said, her eyes wide with dread.

Kral stood. "My prism has arrived."

Dorn was first through the entryway, his gaze streaking across the room, undoubtedly seeking threats. When his survey of the room reached Amy, his eyes flared a brilliant green. A muscle along his jaw began to twitch.

Nuar pushed past him, then quickly started clearing

more space on the floor next to Amy. Lar and Bron followed.

"What happened to our door?" Becca asked.

"Vaporized," Kral said.

Her mouth dropped open, but then she snapped it shut.

"I've scanned the place," Kral said. "They're gone."

Dorn headed to the front of the house, taking up a position near the door where he could also keep an eye on the group. Lar came to stand at Kral's side.

"I need to know what happened here," Kral said. "Bron, survey the house. Check everything. Scan for... residue."

Bron's gaze darted to his.

Kral leaned in close and murmured, "There was another of Becca's sisters here."

"Sophie?" Lar asked.

"Yes," Kral said.

Lar's lips parted as if he was about to say something. He looked back to the two sisters who remained and snapped his mouth shut. His eyes gleamed as bright as the golden sun of Earth's system.

Buddy had been so worried about his family being in danger if he introduced his family to Kral and the others. How had he known? Why hadn't Kral listened? He could have at least taken more steps to keep Becca and her sisters safe.

And now... What would he tell Buddy? How could

Kral explain this to him?

Kral pushed the questions from his mind. He had to focus on the problems before him.

"Bron, report back to me as soon as you're done," Kral said.

Bron nodded, then marched through the debris. He held his arm up before him as his wristband scanned everything in much more detail than Kral had had time for.

As soon as Bron set to his task, Kral hummed a note to reopen communications with the *Arrow*.

"Tarn," he said.

"What do you need?"

"Dispatch a fully armed, cloaked drone to Buddy's parents' house," Kral said. "No more surprises. I want them protected."

"Done."

Kral ended the communication. He couldn't think of other possible targets at the moment aside from Hayley, and he didn't know where she was. Hopefully both her traveling and her tangential relationship with Buddy's family would keep her safe for the moment.

Kral turned back to Becca and Amy, watching Nuar work. Becca's anguish hung between them, thickening the air. He could sense it.

He thought back to what had passed between them on the street outside. There could be no more doubt in his mind as to the truth.

She was his soulmate—and someone had attacked her family. They had injured Amy.

And Sophie… He couldn't think of what had happened to her.

Even if Becca hadn't been Kral's soulmate, Buddy was his friend. An honorary member of their prism.

Kral would find whoever had done this. And when he did, he would make them pay.

Chapter Nine

She could barely breathe. Her baby sister was hurt and Sophie was—

Becca shook the thought from her mind before letting herself finish it. Sophie would be fine. She had to be. Becca didn't think she could handle it if she wasn't.

One of Kral's prism was crouched next to them. He had short brownish-blond hair, lightly tanned skin, and a smile that would probably reassure most people.

Becca would've been more reassured if he didn't have bright red eyes.

Red. Eyes. His irises glowed, just like Kral's.

What the hell was going on here?

Kral's "medical officer," as he'd called him, did the same hand waving thing that Kral had done over Amy's body earlier, but this time, the guy clanged his wristbands together beforehand.

She remembered Kral banging his wristbands together before they entered the house. What were those things?

Becca glanced over to the other men filling her living room. They had the same metal circles on both wrists and they all managed to pull them off, with their muscled physiques and odd aura of...she wasn't quite sure what yet.

They were also all in jeans and boots and T-shirts—aside from Dorn. From the look of it, they shopped at the same store. And bought the same things. Their shirts were even the same powder blue.

It was almost like a uniform. After what Kral had said earlier, Becca wouldn't be surprised if it actually was and this was their "civilian look."

"Don't worry," the medic said. "Your sister will be better than new when I'm done with her."

"Nuar," Kral said. "Address her injuries only."

Nuar—yet another weird name—shook his head. "Nope. My scans have revealed a few genetic anomalies that I can't leave be. There's also a weakness in one of the valves of her heart that could lead to complications in fifty or sixty years. What kind of healer would I be if I let those go?"

"Wait, you can see all that with your...scanner-thing?" Becca said.

Nuar cast a disarming smile at her. Of course, it made her defenses amp up. The only person who seemed able to slip past them was Kral.

"That and more," Nuar said. "It looks like base-level pollution in your environment has caused some damage to a few key systems. I'll be sure to address that as well."

"Why doesn't everybody have access to this?" Becca said. "It isn't right for the government to keep this technology for their soldiers and—"

"We don't work for your government," Kral said.

"What?" Becca had assumed they were soldiers for her country. If they weren't... "Are you spies? Is Buddy caught up in some sort of espionage?"

"Nothing like that," Kral said.

"We aren't spies, we're warriors." Nuar rolled out a thick piece of clear plastic next to Amy. It was wider and longer than she was.

He let out a strange breath, and the plastic sheet snapped up off the carpet, hardening into a flat surface.

"What the hell?" Becca said.

Nuar just smiled at her again. She was either starting to like him or starting to hate him. She hadn't decided yet.

"Portable medical transport," Nuar said. "Could I get some help, please?"

Becca felt Kral grasp her arms and pull her to her feet. He urged her to move out of the way, even though her legs didn't seem to want to take her anywhere.

Dorn appeared next to them. "Let me," he said.

Kral nodded, then put his arm around Becca and tucked her into his side. She wrapped her arm around his waist and held on.

Dorn knelt at Amy's side. When he touched her, his eyes widened and he sucked in a breath. He tightened his lips into a line, brow furrowing, and cast a quick glance around the room, his gaze locking with Becca's for a moment.

What the hell was that all about?

The others didn't seem to have noticed. Dorn quickly turned back to Amy and helped Nuar carefully lift her onto the strange mat, supporting her body evenly. Their hands were so huge compared to Amy's body, it made her seem even more frail.

That wound on her chest...

Her shirt was scorched. Becca couldn't tell if the charred area was just fabric or if parts of it was Amy's skin. A dark stain also spread from the area. If it was blood... There was so much of it.

Becca covered her mouth with her hand to suppress a sob. She blinked back tears.

Crying wouldn't help anything or anyone, but dammit, this was too much. Even for her.

Kral hugged her tighter against his side.

"She's my baby sister," Becca said, almost choking on the words.

"And we will treat her as one of our own." Kral wrapped both arms around her.

The...what had Nuar called it? Portable medical something? The fancy mat started to glow. Crystalline structures sprouted from its sides and quickly grew, curving over Amy's body and encasing her.

"What…" Becca began. "What the hell is it doing?"

"It's putting her in stasis," Nuar said. "And beginning the healing process."

"That doesn't make any sense." Becca had never seen anything like this. It didn't seem possible, even though she was seeing it with her own eyes.

For a moment, she thought maybe this was all fake, staged for some sick reason. She'd seen Amy's wounds from right up close, though. She knew they were real.

But the rest of it?

The crystal shell surrounding Amy filled with golden light that thrummed up and down her body in waves. The lines around her eyes eased. It looked like she wasn't in pain anymore. Her chest still rose and fell, reassuring Becca.

Nuar and Dorn stood.

"She's out of danger while she's in the stasis chamber," Nuar said. "But I can't do more here. I need to get her to the ship."

"And I need to know what's going on." Becca managed to pull herself away from Kral. She turned and glared at them all. "What ship? What happened here? Where's Sophie? Who did this? And how the hell do you have these…gadgets and things? Nobody has technology like this."

Kral and Lar exchanged looks. Becca crossed her arms and amped up her glare.

"Perhaps we should leave you two alone to discuss this," Lar said.

"There's no time." Dorn clanged his wristbands together and the medical mat thing started...floating.

Floated right up off the ground, with Amy laying on it as peaceful as could be.

Meanwhile, Becca was freaking out.

"What the fuck?" She put her hands on the crystal encasing her sister, trying to make sure the thing didn't keep floating up to the ceiling.

"She's all right," Kral said. "It's just the anti-gravity function."

Becca tilted her head to look at him over her shoulder. She hoped he was picking up on the "anti-anymore-bullshit" function she was trying to broadcast from her glare.

"We need to get her to the ship," Kral said. "Both of you, until we can figure out what's going on."

"The ship," Becca said.

What kind of ship?

She wanted to ask, but wasn't sure how much more she could take.

Amy was hurt. Becca could see how bad it was. And Sophie was missing.

What was Becca supposed to do? How could she protect anyone when she was dealing with things so far outside her concept of *reality*?

She would have been a lot worse off if she'd just met these guys herself. But Buddy had been hanging out with them for months. He trusted them. That went a long way in Becca's book.

Whatever Buddy had gotten himself wrapped up in, she still wanted to know what the hell was going on. Apparently, Kral did, too. At least when it came to what had happened here.

Even more than him taking charge and having his team —his prism—investigate their place, she could see it in his eyes. He wasn't going to let this go.

Neither was she.

Becca stood and nodded, but kept one hand on the shell above Amy. Lar had found one of Dash's leashes and attached it to her collar and was leading the dog toward the door.

They all headed into the back yard. The other new guy —Bron—exited last, walking through the empty space that used to be their sliding glass door. It was almost a good thing the glass was gone. The guy was built like a tank, even compared to the others.

A mix of dread and excitement was building in Becca as she looked around for their ship. Maybe it was some sort of super-advanced helicopter? Why would he call it a ship, though?

Maybe it was a land boat.

That was ridiculous. But what kind of ship would be

this far inland? She'd only heard "ship" used with air or water craft.

Well, and spaceships.

Her breath stuck in her chest for a moment, her heart freezing in place. She forced the breath out and kept moving forward.

Don't be ridiculous.

But then Kral led her to a large disc floating a few inches above the grass. Floating. Just like Amy's portable medical thingie.

Was this their ship? Just a giant flying…surfboard?

That was not what Becca had been expecting in any level of her imaginings. Even with the floating, it was a little anti-climactic.

Lar picked up Dash and stepped onto the disc. Nuar followed with Amy. Kral urged Becca to step up onto it as well.

"Nice ship," Becca said. "It's going to be kind of crowded when the other guys join us, though."

Kral smirked. "This isn't my ship and they won't be taking the platform up."

"Up?" Becca asked.

Kral held her gaze as he pointed above them, his smile deepening. Becca slowly craned her head back, her eyes growing wider as she did.

A giant crystal was floating above them. It was bigger than their house.

Light from the street lamp out front glinted off its many facets. More ambient light reflected off sharp angles that jutted out from the main body of the...ship.

This was his ship.

Oh my God...

The ship itself was putting off light as well, but only from a small circular area directly above them. The light trailed down in a tight cylinder that looked just like the cheesey sci-fi movies she'd watched all her life with her family.

"This is..." Her voice trailed off. She didn't want to say it. It was crazy enough that she was thinking it, but saying it? No way.

She didn't have to, though.

"This is a Cygnian vessel," Kral said.

"Cygnian." She nodded as if that made sense, even though she had no idea what it meant.

Okay, she had *some* idea. She just couldn't believe it.

"So, you're from..." Again, she let her voice trail off.

"The Cygnus X-3 system," he said. He pointed to a cluster of stars just above her neighbor's house.

"Oh," Becca said.

Lar stepped closer, Dash still in his arms. "We need to go."

"I know." Kral nodded toward the men standing at the side of the platform.

First Bron, then Dorn leapt up into the air, landing just

inside the ship on the lip of the open circle above them. Thirty feet above them. They didn't even bother grabbing the edge to hoist themselves up.

"How…" Her mouth was dry. She swallowed and tried again. "How did they do that?"

"Cygnus-Prime has an intense gravitational field," Kral said. "Earth is considered a low-gravity world for us."

Earth.

As in, the planet. Her planet.

Not theirs.

"Our physiology had to adapt," Nuar said. "We're much stronger and sturdier than the life forms you're familiar with."

"Life forms." She nodded. "Okay."

She was through the looking glass. Down the rabbit hole. Had taken the red pill. Or was it blue?

It didn't matter.

This was happening. It was real. And the way she saw it, she had two choices.

She could freak out and think she'd gone crazy. Hell, maybe she *had* gone crazy.

But if she was crazy, she couldn't help anyone.

And that brought her to her second option. She could stuff down all the screaming "What the fucks!" going through her head and help her sisters.

Thinking of it like that, it wasn't really a choice at all.

"What are we waiting for?" Becca said. "Let's take

care of Amy and figure out where Sophie is."

Kral's chest seemed to grow even more massive. Was he puffing his chest out? Normally, she would think of it as posturing, but on him it looked more like pride.

The platform they were standing on started to rise. Within seconds, they had joined the others in a large, open room.

She blinked against the brightness, shielding her eyes as they tried to adapt. Colors shimmered across the otherwise milky-white walls, reminding her of her Aunt Libby's favorite opal earrings. Every part of the ship she could see seemed to be made of shimmering surfaces.

Dash was whining next to her, blinking rapidly. Lar held the dog closer to his chest.

"I don't know if you're trying to go with the stereotypes, but can you dim the lights in here?" she said.

Kral looked up and the lights dimmed to a tolerable level. The shimmer on the walls retreated to a simple sheen.

"Stereotypes?" Lar asked.

"Alien abduction stories." Becca was proud at how steady her voice sounded. She also reminded herself that she had chosen to come aboard, not been abducted. "They're usually pictured with the humans being in rooms that are so brightly lit, they can't really see anything."

"Interesting." Nuar started pushing the pallet with Amy's unsettlingly still form on it up a long, curving hallway. Becca followed. "Humans actually have a rather high tolerance for light. Cygnians are one of the few species who can handle even more lumens comfortably."

"'Yay, Earth,' I guess," Becca said.

She glanced behind them as they headed up the sloping corridor. The floor had sealed beneath them. No turning back now.

"The higher radiation levels on Cygnus-Prime caused us to evolve to be able to perceive a wide variety of optical wavelengths," Lar said.

"Plus, almost everything on the planet is made of crystal formations," Kral said. Becca looked over at him and he smiled. "Light does absolutely spectacular things."

"I'd like to see that some day," she said.

His smile softened. "Perhaps one day you will."

That smile of his could almost make her forget her troubles. Almost. But following behind Amy and not knowing where Sophie was…

Becca was on a knife's edge. She had to keep her focus on her situation, yet not let herself think too hard about it. If she did, she'd lose it.

"You're sure you can help her?" she said, walking a little faster so she was more even with Nuar.

"Absolutely." He rested his hand gently on top of the crystal shell encasing Amy. "She won't even have any scarring."

Becca hadn't thought of that. She just wanted her baby

sister well and breathing.

Sophie would be freaking out about scars. Amy would probably think they'd give her bragging rights at the bar.

"Send all the data from your diagnostics and procedures to my wristbands," Bron said, from the back of their group.

Nuar's brow furrowed. "Why?"

"I need to complete my analysis of what happened," Bron said.

"Stream a live feed of the medical bay to the common room as well," Kral said. "I want to monitor your progress with Amy while Bron reconstructs the attack using our holo-emitters."

The attack. It had been an attack. But who would go after her sisters and why?

"Do you have any idea who did this?" Becca asked.

"I only know who we're supposed to suspect," Bron said.

"What the hell does that mean?" she said.

"That he's still analyzing the data." Kral gestured to an archway that led to a large, open room. Nuar kept walking up the hallway, Dorn a few paces behind him.

Becca paused, torn once more between going with Amy and staying with Kral. She couldn't believe how comforting his presence already was. Especially now that she knew what he was.

That he wasn't...human.

Bron walked into the circular chamber. They were going to have a live feed from Nuar's work on Amy. That would have to be enough. There was nothing Becca could do to help her now, but she could maybe help find her other sister.

She followed Kral and Lar into the room. Lar was still carrying Dash.

"You can put her down now," Becca said.

Lar hugged the dog closer again. "She's frightened."

"She gets heavy." Becca knew from experience. Dash wanted to be treated like the family's pom-poms, up to and including being on their laps and sometimes even being carried around.

Lar smirked at her. "She's but a breeze."

Becca's heart gave a little lurch. If she were to judge Kral by the company he kept, he was definitely a good guy. But then, she already knew that, since he was besties with Buddy.

Kral stood to one side, his arms crossed over his massive chest as he stared toward the empty space in the center of the circular room. "What do we know?"

Bron stepped forward. He clanged his wristbands together, and the center of the room filled with lines of bright light. The lines coalesced into a transparent, 3-D view of their house.

Whoa...

"The assailants entered the house through the back

door," Bron said. "All other entry points were intact when we arrived except for the glass door, which had been vaporized."

"The front door was unlocked," Becca said.

The men turned to her with their freaky, overly saturated gazes. Now that she was looking from one to the other of them, they all had eye colors that were way too vibrant to be natural.

For humans, anyway.

It was weirdly disappointing that their eyes were the only thing about them that seemed different. Well, aside from their enormous size, sharp teeth, and all those abs.

"Do you think that Amy and Sophie let whoever is responsible for this walk into their home?" Lar asked.

Becca was pleased Lar didn't suggest that Sophie had tried to run out the front to get away. Becca had to admit that she had considered the thought, but then immediately dismissed it.

There was no way Sophie would have left Amy behind. Not if she had any choice in the matter.

"I'm saying that whoever did this could have picked the lock or made a duplicate of a key or done any number of things to get inside," Becca said. When Lar angled his head at her, she added, "Amy watches lots of crime shows. You pick up stuff."

"Before anyone else moves back into that house, I want us to install a proper security system," Kral said.

"I'm sure Dorn is already designing it." Bron turned back to the hologram floating in the middle of the room and the display changed, zooming in on their living room. Was he controlling it with his mind?

"The energy signature of Amy's wound is the same as weapons used by Coalition soldiers," Bron said.

"The Coalition?" Kral took a very menacing step forward. Bron didn't flinch, raising him in Becca's esteem.

"Why would the Coalition attack Amy?" Lar said. "And why would they take Sophie?"

Of all the questions circling in her mind, one was rising above them all. One she didn't want to ask, but she had to know the answer to.

"We're sure they took Sophie, right?" she asked, her voice thready. "I mean, with all the technology you guys have here, I'm assuming they could have just... just..."

She pinched her eyes shut, trying not to think of all the movies with rayguns that she and her family had watched. One shot, and the poor victim would turn into a glowing outline and then a pile of ash.

They'd already vaporized her sliding glass door.

But those were movies and this was reality. A reality with spaceships and antigravity platforms and...and aliens.

And Kral.

He was at her side suddenly. Somehow, she sensed his approach without even opening her eyes.

He wrapped his arms around her and crushed her to his

chest. She clung to him, not knowing where else to turn, and honestly, not wanting to turn elsewhere, even though she didn't understand it.

Chapter Ten

"Continue your report," Kral said.

Bron nodded. "Our energy scans didn't detect anything strong enough to be a disintegration field."

Becca tightened her grip on Kral. Her voice was muffled when she spoke, her face still pressed against his chest. "That's reassuring. I guess."

"We will find your sister," Kral said. "If they wanted to kill her, they would have done so immediately."

"That's *not* reassuring." Becca leaned back so she could glare up at him.

That knowledge would have comforted him. But Earthlings were not like Cygnians. He had learned that during his friendship with Buddy.

"Then know that we will not stop until we have found whoever is behind this and brought them to justice," Kral said. Perhaps that would help her feel better.

"I'm only concerned with getting my sister back safely. Both of them." Becca looked over to Lar. "Do you know if things are going well with Amy?"

"Nuar's data stream has indicated no issues," Lar said.

Another hologram that was running next to him grew larger in size, showing Nuar working over Amy in the healing crystal. Dorn was standing nearby.

"We should focus our efforts on tracking Sophie," Bron said. He hummed the note to shrink the hologram from the medical bay. "Whoever took her doesn't have much of a head start."

"We should contact the *Reckoning*," Lar said. "And demand they return her."

"Wait, you know who has her?" Becca turned back to Kral. "Who is the Reckoning?"

"You mean 'what,'" Kral said. "The *Reckoning* is a Coalition warship."

"And they're bad guys?" she asked. "The Coalition?"

Kral's spine plates tingled, along with his fingertips. Not long ago, he would have said yes. Now, he wasn't certain.

"There are those among them who are immoral," Kral said.

"That's everywhere," Becca said. "Do they have the means to do this? The motive?" She let out a little exasperated noise. "Wow, I really am watching too many crime shows with Amy."

"Your line of inquiry is sound," Bron said. "Coalition soldiers could easily have taken your sister. And the energy signature on Amy's injury matches Coalition technology."

"We should disable their ship before they realize we know of their treachery," Lar said. "Let them see how easy it would be for us to destroy them."

Becca sucked in a breath. She pushed away from Kral and stalked over to Lar. Though she looked tiny next to the Cygnian, she showed no signs of being intimidated. The fact that he was still holding Dash might have helped.

"Sophie might be alive on that ship," Becca said. "Nobody's destroying anything."

"I said disable, not destroy," Lar said. "We are a warrior race. Fighting is second nature to us."

"If you need to hit something, then go find your... space gym or something," Becca said. "Nobody attacks anything until we have Sophie back safely. Unless, you know, we have to attack the people who have her. Okay, fine, I see your point."

"Attacking the *Reckoning* is a last resort," Kral said. "There's always a chance that one of our friends from Harbor is on board. Or even Buddy or his mate."

"Buddy?" Becca turned toward him.

"Nika is a Coalition soldier," Kral said. "The highest ranking engineer in the entire fleet. They are sometimes on the *Reckoning* when they're together."

"My brother is dating an alien." Becca angled her head and stared at the wall.

"Is it so odd to think of an Earthling becoming involved with an alien?" Kral asked, his throat oddly tight.

Many humans had pair bonded with Sadirian mates over the last Earth year. They didn't seem to think it was strange at all.

But Kral didn't really care what they thought. He wanted to know what Becca thought.

"Seeing as how I didn't even know aliens existed until a few minutes ago, it's probably going to take me a little while to get used to the idea," she said. "No wonder he's been so secretive about it. Our parents are going to freak."

Kral did his best to hide his disappointment. Up to now, she'd given every indication that she was as drawn to him as he was to her. Maybe he'd been projecting his own feelings upon her, though.

She just needed time. They all did.

He wondered how long his people would need to reconcile themselves to the idea of having an Earthling as their future queen.

His thoughts were tying themselves in knots, his emotions tangled as he tried to sort through the feelings raging in him. Honor his people or follow his hearts?

Right now, he needed to focus on Sophie.

"If Nika is part of the Coalition, then they can't be involved," Becca said. "Buddy would never be involved with someone who could do something like this."

"And there is no reason for the Coalition to take Sophie," Kral said.

"The evidence we have points to them." Lar set down

Dash and stalked up to Kral, a clear challenge in his gaze that Kral didn't quite understand.

Kral met his approach, curling his hands into fists. He wished he could let Lar cut loose on him, to get out some of whatever energy was unnerving him, but then Becca would see things Kral wasn't ready for her to see.

Instead of striking Lar or tossing him across the room to help them fight off their anxious energy, Kral reached out and gripped Lar's shoulders.

"Calm yourself, brother," Kral said. "The Coalition knows of our bond with Buddy and that we would see an attack on his family as an act of war. They stand to gain nothing by this and have much to lose."

"We must get Sophie back." Again, the intensity in Lar's voice surprised Kral. "We are sworn to protect her and all of Buddy's family."

"If the Coalition doesn't have anything to gain through this, then who does?" Becca asked. "Or who would benefit from you thinking that the Coalition is behind it?"

Warmth built in Kral's hearts. Becca was as intelligent as she was fierce.

Kral stepped away from Lar and said, "That is where I think we'll find our answers."

"It isn't easy to obtain a Coalition bracer," Bron said.

"Which is exactly what they want us to think." Kral looked to Bron and said, "The green blood on Dash?"

"It's from a Tau Ceti, as I'm sure you suspected," Bron

said. "The scouts have red blood to help them fit in among Earthlings. Dash must have faced a cybernetically enhanced soldier."

"A Tau Ceti cyborg?" Lar's eyes widened as he looked at the green-tinged fur around Dash's muzzle and down her chest. His look of awe turned to a smile as he examined the dog. "It looks like Dash fought bravely and well."

"My reconstruction is ready." Bron hummed a note and the holoprojection began to move. It showed the glass partition flash with a bright light just before three figures entered the living room. Their features were blurred, but they all wore Coalition uniforms.

Dash leapt for the first one across the threshold, biting their arm. The silver fabric of his uniform would protect him somewhat from energy weapons, but Coalition uniforms were primarily for helping them survive the vacuum of space for short periods of time. They so rarely were involved in physical confrontations, their uniforms didn't protect against them.

The three figures aimed at the dog, but she was able to evade their blasts and run out the doorway. Then, they turned their weapons on the sisters.

They aimed for Sophie, but Amy threw herself in the way. The blast hit her in the chest, throwing her into a bookcase. The impact knocked it off balance, toppling it over on top of her. Sophie ran toward her sister, picking up books and throwing them at the nearest assailant.

"How do you know she did that?" There was a tremor in Becca's voice. "I mean, it seems like something she'd do, but…"

"The scatter pattern of the books didn't match how they would have landed from the bookshelf being overturned," Bron said.

"I guess that makes sense." Becca was staring intently at the simulation. Kral wasn't sure if it was helping her or making her fear worse.

The projection kept going, showing a fourth person who stood near Sophie. The figure grabbed her and dragged her through the house toward the front door. Sophie slumped against them.

"What makes you think she was incapacitated?" Kral asked.

"There weren't enough signs of struggle for me to think otherwise," Bron said. "The question isn't whether she was incapacitated or not, but how it was managed. There was no energy signature from a stun blast or a Coalition stasis disk."

"He could have just knocked her out," Becca said, her voice tight.

The men all turned to look at her.

"You know, a blow to the head." She hugged herself, rubbing one of her arms as she spoke. "That will knock most Earthlings unconscious."

"Really?" Bron said. "No wonder Buddy is always warning us to be careful with him."

"We need to bring Buddy in on this," Becca said.

Kral bristled. "Do you think we can't handle the matter?"

"How the hell should I know?" she yelled. "You can all jump really high and your technology is beyond anything I've ever seen before, but that doesn't mean you're the top dogs of the universe."

Dash's ears perked up. Becca raised her hand, with her palm flat, and said, "Settle down, girl. You're not the top dog, either, except when it comes to agility challenges."

Bron crossed his arms over his chest, staring at Becca. No doubt, he wished to prove to her that she was wrong. Kral felt the urge as well. He fought it back.

"Becca is right," Kral said.

"I am?" Her eyes widened a bit as she stared at him.

"We might be one of the strongest life forms in the galaxy, but our technology is no match for the Vegans'," Kral said. "Lyrians are even harder to kill than us. There are innumerable sentients with special abilities beyond what we can do—Antareans with their wings and Scorpiians with their shape-shifting."

"Shape-shifting?" Becca said. "Really?"

Kral nodded.

She shook herself as if she'd caught a chill, then said, "That's actually not what I was talking about. I'm talking about information. We're not going to find Sophie by hitting things. Probably. Hitting people, maybe, but only the ones who might know what's going on."

Bron stared at her for a few moments, then said, "She makes a good point. We need more information. The Coalition bracer used in this attack had to come from somewhere."

Lar bared his teeth in a smile that promised battle. "Perhaps we should pay a visit to the *Reckoning* after all."

"Inform them of our arrival," Kral said. He struck his wristbands together and hummed the note for the ship's communication channel. "Rom, set an intercept course for the *Reckoning*."

"Easy enough," Rom said, "since they're just sitting on the far side of Earth's moon."

Kral suppressed a growl. "Just do it. Tarn, make sure our cloak is holding. Nuar, be aware that we're leaving Earth's orbit."

"Understood," Nuar said.

"As if our cloak wouldn't hold," Tarn said over the open comm channel.

"Can Nuar hear me?" Becca stepped closer to Kral.

"Yes," Kral said.

Staring up at the ceiling, Becca asked, "Is Amy okay?"

"She's still in stasis," Nuar said. "The level of tissue damage to her chest was extreme and there were a few other…issues. It will take some time for her to recover."

"But she will recover, right?" Becca asked.

"I haven't lost anyone yet," Nuar said.

Becca let out a breath, her shoulders relaxing a bit. She closed her eyes and bowed her head.

Over the comm, they heard Tarn snort. "You've only ever worked on Cygnians. And we're nearly indestructible."

Becca's eyes flew open, her gaze snapping to Kral.

Kral was going to go down to engineering and chuck Tarn into the reactor core.

"Tarn, stop being an ass," Bron said. He walked over to Becca and actually placed a hand on her shoulder. "Your sister will be fine. Even without the technology of our vessel, Nuar is a skilled healer."

Becca cast a weak smile at Bron. He looked over to Kral and nodded.

Kral's hearts filled with gratitude. For Bron to reach out to her and try to bring her comfort was yet another sign that she was Kral's soulmate.

Nuar had found his soulmate on Earth. If Kral had found his here as well, they all had hope.

But even if Becca was his soulmate, she was also an Earthling. Aside from the challenges they would have with his own people, he had to wonder how she would adapt to everything she was learning. She hadn't even seen him— or any of the Cygnian warriors—as they truly appeared.

His prism was accepting Becca. But would she accept

them?

Chapter Eleven

The hologram display thing filled the center of the room, giving Becca a detailed view of the warship they were approaching. The very big warship, if everything was to scale.

Kral's ship, which she'd been told was called the *Arrow*, was heading toward one of the hangar bays. It *fit* in one of the hangar bays. Easily. And Kral's ship was bigger than Becca's house.

The *Reckoning* must be as big as a city.

It was long and kind of blocky compared to the Cygnian ship. There were gun ports all over it and big thrusters at the back.

Somebody has a complex.

She couldn't deny that the ship looked intimidating. But if she could hold her own with half a dozen huge, apparently indestructible Cygnians, she wasn't going to let this ship get under her skin.

Mostly.

Curiosity was better than fear. She tried to focus on wondering what sort of aliens she might see on board a vessel this size. There had to be thousands living there.

So far, she was kind of disappointed with how mundane everyone looked. Granted, Kral and his prism were unbelievably hot. But they just looked like hot humans. Enormous humans, but still.

Nika looked human, too.

Where were the robots or ant-people? Where were the Grays? Nobody even had so much as pointed ears, for crying out loud.

She tore her gaze away from the visual of their approach to stare at Kral. Okay, it wasn't that hard to look at him instead.

Her eyes gravitated to him whenever she wasn't focusing on something. He'd already caught her staring at him half a dozen times. Each time, he'd smirked at her and turned his attention back to what he was doing.

That cocky smirk should have set her off. Instead, it set her smoldering.

There was nothing disappointing about Kral. In fact, through all of this, he had been the one point of light that guided her. The rock-solid foundation that made her feel like she wasn't losing her feet—or her mind.

There was something between them. Something strong and strange. She didn't understand it.

Maybe it was part of his alien nature. He could be more different than she realized, but in a way she couldn't see.

Which gave her an idea.

"I'm going to go check on Amy before we go," Becca

said. "Don't leave the ship without me."

If Kral thought her statement was abrupt, he didn't mention it. Instead, he took a few steps closer and said, "I can take you to our medical bay."

"No need." She glanced at Bron and Lar, who were both staring at her. "I mean, Dash can show me the way."

"The dog?" Lar lifted an eyebrow.

"Sophie trained her," Becca said. "Check it out." She leaned down and patted her thighs, hoping this time Dash would actually listen to her. She mostly only listened to Sophie. "Here girl."

Dash had been lying at Lar's feet. She seemed to really like the guy. When Becca called, Dash sprang into the air, then ran to Becca and started barking.

"Shh, settle down." Becca petted Dash's neck until the dog calmed a bit, then said, "Find Amy."

Dash's ears perked up, then she turned and ran out of the room.

"Leave without me, and I'll kick your asses," Becca called over her shoulder as she chased the border collie. She could hear their laughter following her along the hall.

Dash lived up to her name, making Becca run after her. The medical bay wasn't far, thankfully. Dash turned down a couple of corridors, then ran into a small room.

"What's this?" Nuar was sitting in a chair that looked like it was made of glass. It was probably crystal instead, like everything else in the ship.

Dash ran up to him, wagging her tail. Nuar bent down to pet the dog, a huge smile on his face. It brightened further when he looked up at Becca.

Damn, she was really starting to like these guys.

"I wanted to check on Amy before we go aboard the *Reckoning*," Becca said. She walked to the tall table where Amy was sleeping.

A crystal shell still surrounded her sister. Gold light filled the chamber, with more intense lines of brightness sweeping up and down the length of her body. Even more beams were directed at her chest and shoulder.

Her clothes were gone, but she'd been covered with a sparkly cobalt blue blanket. The table beneath her had some sort of cloth covering as well in the same color.

Nuar came to stand behind Becca. She had to clear her throat before she could speak. When she did, her voice was tight.

"She looks comfortable."

"She's healing well," Nuar said. "Your sister is strong."

"I know it." Becca stared at Amy's face for a few moments. "None of us was expecting her, least of all my folks. She's ten years younger than Sophie, but never lets that stop her from getting in our faces when we have it coming. She never tried to keep up with us, either. Always did her own thing."

Becca reached out and touched the crystal shell. It was warm and made her fingers tingle.

She snatched her hand away and looked at Nuar. "Sorry. I probably shouldn't have done that."

"It's not a problem." He smiled at her kindly, then placed his own hand on the shell above Amy's head. "Cygnians have a need to be close to our loved ones as well. Especially in times like this."

Becca nodded, then placed her hand back on the crystal. "Does she know I'm here?"

"Probably not. Her mind is in a very low level of activity while her body heals."

"I suppose that's for the best." Becca turned to Nuar, letting her hands drop to her sides.

"But you have another reason for coming here," he said.

"I... Yeah." Becca scrambled for words. Dash looked up at her, giving her an idea to stall. "Could you watch over Dash for me? While we're on the *Reckoning*? I mean, I'm assuming you'll stay here."

"Of course." Nuar knelt next to Dash and scratched behind her ears. "I'd love the company."

"Thanks." Becca shifted her weight from one foot to another.

"And what else do you need from me?"

"What? Nothing. I—"

Nuar laughed, still petting Dash.

"You and Buddy are very alike," he said. "When something is important to you, you have trouble expressing it."

Her breath caught in her chest, and she again felt herself scrambling for words. "I don't…"

She shook her head. He was right. This guy—this *alien* guy—that she'd only just met already had her number.

"Okay, fine," she said. "I do have a question."

"Hopefully, I have an answer." He stood, waiting patiently.

"Do you guys… I mean… Are you…"

"Are we physiologically compatible with humans?"

How the hell did he know she was going to ask that?

"Absolutely." He opened his mouth to speak, then he cringed and snapped it shut. What had he been about to say?

Looking somewhat sheepish, he continued. "Rom would be the best source for details on that. He's been amassing quite the experience with Earth women during our stay."

"What? No, no. That's not…"

Her mind kind of stalled as his words fully registered. Rom was having sex with Earthlings?

He was super-hot, like all the guys in Kral's prism. Becca was sure there would be a line of women happy to have one-night-stands with him, alien or not. But Becca was looking for something more permanent.

Was Kral?

"Do you guys put out some kind of pheromones or

something?" she blurted.

"Pheromones?" For the first time, Nuar's smile faltered. He shook his head.

"You know, like... To attract a mate."

Damn, her cheeks were tingling. She must be blushing. If Amy could see Becca now, she'd never hear the end of it.

Nuar's lips pinched together, as if he was trying not to smile. "No, we don't work that way. Our bodies are designed to be as impermeable as possible. It's what makes our skin so hard and our muscles so dense. The natural shielding we've evolved also keeps things from escaping, I guess you'd say."

That answered one of her questions, but opened up about a thousand more. Nuar kept going, his tone gentle and almost reverent.

"There is something we experience with our mates, though," he said. "Or rather, our one true mate. An experience we share."

Becca's interest perked way more than it should have. "What's that?"

Nuar's smile deepened. "Our planet is protected by a crystal shell. It filters out much of the radiation and intense gravity of the black hole nearby."

"You guys live near a black hole?"

He shrugged. "It's made us strong. The shell also transforms some of the radiation into the light and warmth that enables life to exist on our world."

"Wow. That's really cool."

"You'd have to talk to Bron about the exact science behind it—he's our science officer. But in terms of Cygnian physiology, I can tell you that our people have evolved to have complex ways of interacting with each other and our environment. Instead of pheromones, our bodies communicate through vibrations."

Becca arched an eyebrow. The urge to make a joke was so strong.

"Go on," she said.

"We believe that each soul vibrates on a particular frequency. Not just Cygnians, but the soul of every life form in the galaxy. When you find others who exist on a similar wavelength, you can forge soul bonds."

"Is that like what you and Kral and the others have with your prism?"

Nuar's smile brightened. "Exactly. We are incredibly fortunate that we found a complete prism. It takes seven Cygnians to form a full spectrum."

"Spectrum…" Becca raked her brain trying to remember her science classes. "Spectrums deal with light and rainbows or something?"

"Or something." Nuar laughed. "But even beyond the prism bond, there is one even more revered and more rare. The soulmate bond."

Her heart seemed to freeze for a moment, before

starting to pound. Something deep in her stirred and more of those tingles shot up and down her spine. She wasn't sure if it was more exciting or frightening.

"Soulmate bond. What's that?" she asked, trying to make her voice sound casual.

"Some think it's when a Cygnian finds the person who carries the other half of their soul. I believe it's when they find that one person in the universe whose frequency is so in tune with their own that they make the most perfect harmony. We even sometimes call it 'achieving frequency.' We're told we can feel it when it happens—an unmistakeable bond, stronger than any other."

"Wow." A wistful note entered her tone. She cleared her throat to get rid of it. "Like, unmistakable how?"

"The pair is drawn to each other with a pull stronger than Cygnus X—the black hole near our homeworld. We can sense each other's moods and even their locations, thankfully." A haunted look crossed his features briefly, but he shook it off. With a smirk, he added, "And the physical attraction is impossible to resist or ignore. A simple touch sends us spiraling into—"

"You Cygnians are lucky to be able to form bonds with each other like that," she cut in, her mind balking at hearing more on that particular aspect of the topic.

"You would think. But there's a population imbalance on our world. Less than ten percent of our population is female."

"What?" She thought of the planet, imagining it covered with gorgeous men, but only a few equally gorgeous women. "Do the soulmate bonds occur between same genders ever?"

"Sometimes," Nuar said. "But it isn't as common. Usually, those would be prism bonds."

"That sounds really complicated."

Nuar laughed. "And it's only going to become more so."

"What do you mean?"

"We recently discovered that we're compatible with other sentients."

Becca's mouth went dry. "Other sentients?"

"Sadirians, for one," he said. "Like Nika."

"Oh. Any others?"

His smile morphed to a smirk. "Earthlings."

Becca felt like the floor beneath her feet had disappeared and she was free falling. She rested her hand on the crystal shell to steady herself.

"That's good," she heard herself saying. "That'll give you all more options, since you need more women." She laughed, her mouth running off without her brain's permission. "Have you heard of the movie *Mars Wants Women*?"

"No."

"It's a kind of similar situation. Lots of Martian men. Not many ladies. Might want to check that out. Or not. I mean. Your preference."

Why could she not stop talking? This *never* happened to her. Never.

Nuar just kept staring at her with that bemused expression on his face. Becca needed to retreat and regroup.

"I better go join the others before they head out without me," she said. "Not that they would. I mean, I told them not to."

She backed toward the door, distracted by Dash cocking her head at Becca.

"Thanks for taking care of Dash." Becca looked to the crystal encasing her sister, remembering her need to focus. "And Amy."

Becca had to help her sisters. She'd figure out whatever was going on with her and Kral later.

Definitely not a soulmate bond.

Chapter Twelve

How long had it been since Kral stood before the *Arrow's* only hatch that had an actual ramp, watching it descend toward the floor of this very Coalition vessel?

His thoughts wandered back to that monumental event. He and his prism had come seeking retribution, and then he had met Buddy and heard his sisters speak and sing. Kral had heard Becca.

The harmony in their voices stirred something so strong within him that he couldn't ignore it. He didn't want to. Not when Becca's voice had affected him so intensely while she spoke.

He had analyzed their song, lifted out different elements, and discovered Becca's voice within the strains. A voice that had made him feel at once complete and utterly empty when the melody stopped.

Now, she was standing at his side. Even with his doubts, he felt stronger than he ever had before. He looked over to her and took in her nervous expression. He thought he could almost feel her anxiousness, though they hadn't bonded.

Yet.

Reaching over, he took her hand in his and gently squeezed it. She smiled at him and nodded. He released her hand, then turned toward the hatch.

They walked down the ramp together, following Bron, Dorn, and Lar. The warriors had taken up protective stances around Becca, blocking her from view.

The commander of the *Reckoning* awaited them, along with several other Sadirians that Kral didn't recognize. And one that he did.

Vay stood ramrod straight, a deep frown on her face, her brow furrowed, and the rims of her eyes red and swollen. Kral's hearts seized briefly.

He stepped forward and angled his head toward the commander.

"Marq," Kral said.

"Kral." Marq stood motionless, his expression vaguely troubled. "Whatever it is that you need, I hope we can assist. However…"

He glanced over at Vay. "Perhaps in the future, you can let us know before you leave Harbor. The town was created for other sentients to visit Earth and learn of their ways, but the Department of Homeworld Security is adamant that we not give away our presence to other Earthlings yet."

"We are aware of their desire," Kral said. "And have kept our vessel cloaked while traveling."

"Did you also keep it cloaked while hovering over

Becca's house for fifteen minutes earlier tonight?" Vay said, her tone clipped and her eyes shimmering.

Kral turned to Bron, who simply shrugged.

"Do you have any idea what a mess it caused to have her neighbors notice a giant crystal floating above their houses?" Vay nearly shouted.

"We kept the lights off," Bron said. "They couldn't have seen more than a shadow."

"A shadow that half a dozen people filmed and uploaded to the internet," she said. "Our teams have been working for hours tracking everything down and trying to spin it so that humans don't get any more evidence that aliens exist. They saw the hatch open."

That wasn't good. Still, their reaction to the situation irked Kral.

"The Coalition has entire teams dedicated to keeping low-tech planets from gathering evidence of alien existence," he said. "Surely it wasn't too much trouble."

Vay lurched forward, but Marq caught her shoulder.

"Vay," he snapped.

Kral held up a hand. "No, let her approach. Vay is a trusted friend."

She scoffed. "What about *me* trusting *you*? I'm the one who's supposed to keep you in Harbor."

Kral felt the plates on his spine start to rise and fought against it. He turned to Marq and said, "We go where we wish when we wish. You can't hold her responsible for our movements."

"I'm aware," Marq said. "I wish you could convince her of that."

"We aren't the ones who are mandating that people on this planet don't find out about us," she said. "It's the Earthlings we work with who have given that command. This is their home. A home they are choosing to share with *my* people. *You* have a home. We don't."

Kral had never seen Vay so angry. And as he listened to her words, he realized that she had every right to be.

"If the Department of Homeworld Security decides that letting us share the Sol system with them is too dangerous and kick us out, we will have nowhere to go that is safe." She stepped closer, so that she was inches away from him and jabbed a finger into his chest. "Can you comprehend how utterly terrifying that is for us? For me? I will not be the one who makes it so my people have to wander through the void, being constantly hounded—and destroyed—by the Assembly."

"Vay—" Kral began, but Vay cut him off.

"The Coalition has changed," she shouted, tears flowing down her cheeks. "But if you are too stubborn and set in your ways to change as well, then maybe you *shouldn't* be here. I will not allow you to jeopardize my people's future for your whims."

He had wanted to see her temper. He needed to know that the Coalition programming had truly been purged from her mind and that she was her own person. But he had never intended for this.

Even with all the time they'd spent with Buddy, Kral and the others were still adjusting to co-existing with such fragile life forms. He knew their bodies were delicate in comparison with the Cygnians', but not that their homes were just as precarious.

The crystal shielding of Cygnus-Prime was just as impenetrable as the people living within it—aside from a few locations where his people had carved sorts of air locks to allow their ships to travel into space. He couldn't imagine not having his homeworld available as his...well, home.

Kral was beginning to understand the situation of the Sadirians from a new perspective. One he did not like at all.

He put his hands on Vay's shoulders. She angled her chin up and glared at him defiantly. The glimmer in her eyes was too much. He pulled her into a hug, being careful not to crush her.

"I'm sorry, Vay," he said. "I didn't mean to endanger your people. I can explain to the Department of Homeworld Security. The blame lies solely with me, and I will make sure all the Cygnians who visit Earth in the future follow your protocols—including myself."

"Oh." She sniffed against his shoulder. "Well, thank you."

Vay stepped back and quickly wiped at her eyes. Marq reached out and rested his hand on Vay's shoulder. She smiled at him and gave him a brief nod.

The High Council of the Coalition had programmed many of their soldiers to be emotionless. Marq had been one of the Sadirians affected. To see him reach out to Vay —and to see her anger—was reassuring. Still, Kral again felt grateful that the High Council had been destroyed.

"Now that we have settled that matter," Marq said, "what has brought you to the *Reckoning*?"

Kral gestured to his men as he took a step to the side. The four of them made space, bringing Becca into view.

She looked around at each of them, as if surprised to be the center of attention suddenly. Her gaze fixed on Marq and Vay.

"Hey," Becca said.

Vay's face lit up. "Sophie?"

Just as suddenly, her smile vanished, a look of astonishment taking its place, quickly followed by a return of her earlier fury.

"Kraaal!" Vay yelled, dragging out his name in a way he'd never heard.

He stifled a laugh at the amusing sound, not wanting to make things worse. Instead, he coughed.

"This is actually Becca," he said.

"I'm sorry," Vay said. "You both look so alike in the pictures Buddy has shared with us. In the last one I saw,

Sophie was wearing that shirt."

Becca shrugged. "Don't worry about it. Happens all the time. And this is my shirt. Sophie likes to steal it from me." Becca's voice became a bit rough as she spoke.

Kral didn't understand how anyone could possibly mistake the two sisters. Their appearances might be nearly identical, but the women had such different energy. He knew he would be able to tell them apart, even in the flat images Earthlings used to document their histories.

"We don't perform mind-wipes anymore," Marq said, in his flat tone.

Becca's eyes narrowed and her hands curled into fists as she took a step toward Marq. "What-wipes?"

Kral snarled, his spine plates rising beneath the thin fabric of his T-shirt and his claws extending. Luckily, Becca's back was to him and she didn't see. Lar placed a hand on Kral's shoulder, urging him to calm down.

"We aren't here for a mind-wipe," Lar said. "We're here because Becca's sisters were attacked tonight."

Vay gasped.

"Attacked?" Marq said. "How?"

"With Coalition technology," Bron said.

"You can't possibly think that we would—" Vay stopped as Kral held up a hand.

"We know it wasn't you," Kral said, finally bringing his body back under control.

"Oh." Vay's brow furrowed, as if she didn't quite

believe him.

"If you know we aren't behind it, why are you here?" Marq asked.

"Because..." Kral took a deep breath. He did not want to finish his sentence.

Becca looked to him, her eyes pleading, and he knew in that moment that he would do anything for her.

"Because, we need your help," he said.

Marq blinked. Then he blinked again and shook his head.

"I..." He looked over at Vay, who shrugged. "I..."

"Will do everything in our power to assist you," Vay finished for him.

"Yes," Marq said, scowling deeply. He turned to Becca. "Do you have any idea who is behind the attacks?"

"The um..." She glanced over at Kral. "The Tau Yeti?"

This time, Kral did laugh. "The Tau Ceti."

"Yeah, right," Becca said. "Them."

Vay turned to Marq and asked, "Why would the Tau Ceti attack Buddy's sisters?"

"The bigger question is, why would they try to make it look like we did it?" Marq said. "Could it be that rogue Coalition agents are behind it instead?"

"Rogue agents?" Becca asked.

"In our struggles with the Tau Centauran Assembly, we've lost several key facilities," Marq said. "Including our prison colony on Gliese 581d. There were many high-level convicts there, including Sadirians loyal to the High Council."

"And a couple of Tau Ceti operatives I really wish weren't on the loose," Vay added.

"Wait, who is the High Council?" Becca asked.

"They were the asshats that used to rule us," Vay said.

Marq looked puzzled. "Ass-hats?"

Vay waved off his implied question. "It's an Earth expression. Anyway, they ruled most of the galaxy for millennia."

"But not the Cygnus X-3 system," Kral said, taking a deep breath and striking his chest. The other three warriors with him did the same.

"Oh, my God." Becca rolled her eyes. "Enough with the posturing. So, what happened to them?"

Vay's smile faded. She swallowed hard and said, "The Tau Ceti joined forces with the Centaurans. They call themselves the Tau Centauran Assembly. They somehow gained access to super-advanced technology and…"

"And they used it to wipe out every colony, dome-world, and space station in our home system," Marq said. "Including the complete destruction of our planet, Sadr-4."

"Where the High Council lived," Vay finished.

"Damn, that's rough," Becca said. "I'm sorry."

"The High Council deserved their end," Marq said. "But the rest of us are still paying for their crimes. The Assembly seems determined to destroy every home we try to make for our people. And it's a struggle to get other sentients to trust us after their mistreatment by the former Coalition."

"*Our* mistreatment." Vay reached out and touched Marq's arm.

He opened his mouth as if to say something, a strange mix of emotions warring in his expression. But then he shook his head, and the blankness crept back into his features.

Kral thought he could see an edge of something behind that mask. Perhaps there was more hope for Marq than Kral had originally thought.

"Okay, so, some of the prisoners in that place liked how things used to be." Becca started pacing as she spoke.

"And some were Tau Ceti operatives who had assignments on Earth," Vay said. "The Department of Homeworld Security stopped them and turned them over to us, though. None of us thought there was a possibility we'd soon be at war."

"You should have," Becca said. "With just the little you've told me, I'm surprised it didn't happen sooner."

"The High Council used drugs and mental programming pods to control us," Marq said.

Becca stopped abruptly and stared at him, fire flooding her gaze. Her hands curled into fists again and her feet were set in a warrior's stance. She stood that way for long enough that Vay started to fidget.

"Um, do you have more questions?" Vay asked.

"Give me a minute," Becca said. "I'm still calming down."

Kral let out a laugh. Becca started, then turned that glare on him.

"You are as fierce as Pickles," Kral said.

"Pickles." Becca's tone was ice to her gaze's fire. "You're comparing me to a Pomeranian?"

"The fiercest Pomeranian in the galaxy," Kral said.

"Is there anything else I need to know to help sort through this mess?" Each word of Becca's question was clipped.

Vay popped up on her toes. "Oh, you should know that Earth is safe, because it's been colonized by Vegans."

"Vegans." Becca turned toward Vay.

"Yes," Vay said. "It rhymes with 'rayguns.' They're small, reptilian humanoids from the Vega system."

"Lizard-people?" A hint of excitement threaded through Becca's tone. "And they live on Earth?"

"Yes," Vay said.

"Lizard-people…" Becca's eyes were wide as she smiled. "Do they have, like, human suits they dress up in so that we don't know they're reptiles?"

Vay made a face. "Um, no. They use the cloaking devices in their exo-suits to become invisible when needed. I suppose they could use a holo-emitter like the Cygnians, but they'd still be really short."

"Holo-emitter?" Becca turned to Kral, her gaze roving over his body. "Wait, are *you* lizard-people?"

"Of course not, we're Cygnian," Lar said.

"But—" Becca halted as Kral stepped forward.

"None of this is helping us determine who attacked Becca's sisters," Kral said.

"It is, though," Becca said. She held up a finger. "We have a list of suspects. Escaped convicts from the Coalition who want things to go back to the way they were. So, they're crazy enough to do it, obviously."

She held up a second finger. "Or members of the Tau Centauran Assembly who…" She shook her head. "I don't know what their motive would be, since they're already winning the war." She winced and added, "Sorry," glancing at Marq and Vay.

"Whoever did this is trying to damage our relationship with the Cygnians," Marq said. "Which is why I think it *is* rogue Coalition agents, especially since the energy signatures match ours. Why do you suspect the assembly was involved?"

Becca shook her head. "Mostly because Dash was covered in Tau Ceti blood when she found us."

Chapter Thirteen

Marq and Vay both froze at Becca's statement.

"Blood?" Vay asked.

"Yeah, it was all green and stuff." Becca pointed at Kral. "I wouldn't have known what it was if Kral hadn't told me. Of course, when I got to our place and found it trashed, that would have clued me in that something was off."

Her stomach clenched as she remembered their home in shambles. Amy lying on the floor.

If Becca had come home by herself, she would have had no idea what had happened. She wouldn't have been able to help Amy. Amy might have—

Becca tightened her fists, her nails digging into her palms.

Kral *had* been there to help them. Amy was recovering. And Sophie would be fine, too. Once they found her. Becca had to believe that.

"Maybe *we* need more information now," Vay said. "With Kral and his prism with you, I think we kind of assumed whoever attacked you was run off."

"I wasn't there," Becca said. "I was on my way home

from work and I ran into Kral."

Vay made a little grumbling sound.

"Anyway, he was walking me home, but Dash found us." Becca told herself the shiver running through her was because it was drafty in the hangar bay and she was used to the Summer heat of Florida. She didn't believe it, though. "She had this green stuff on her mouth and chest, and Kral said it was Tau Ceti blood."

Bron spoke up behind them. "My analysis confirmed it."

"Well, are Amy and Sophie okay?" Vay asked.

Becca opened her mouth to speak, but only a weird little sound came out. Dammit, she had to hold it together. She had to explain what had happened and get the information they needed to find Sophie and rescue her and —

Kral placed his hand on her shoulder and gave it a gentle squeeze. Dorn, Bron, and Lar also stepped closer, encasing her in a circle of Cygnians.

Part of her wanted to shove them away and say she didn't need them trying to protect her. A deeper part was so grateful they were there.

"We discovered Amy in their home," Kral said. "She had sustained serious injuries."

"A close-range blast from a Coalition weapon," Bron said.

"If Kral hadn't been there and summoned us, she

wouldn't have survived," Lar said.

Becca felt a little woozy. She had suspected Amy's injuries were that severe just looking at them. She'd have been a fool not to. But hearing it out loud made it worse. Made it real.

She wasn't the only one having trouble processing it. Vay covered her mouth with her hand and even Marq actually looked like he wanted to hit something.

"And Sophie?" Marq asked.

"They took her," Becca said.

"And that is why we're here," Kral said. "We haven't been in the Sol system long enough to know the area well. We don't know exactly who could have done this or where they might have taken Sophie. And we still don't know why."

"Then let us work together to find out." Marq turned to Vay and said, "I want Len brought in on this. Have him review all of the data they've gathered up to this point. Our scanners might pick up different variables."

"I'll ask my foster-parents." Vay turned to Becca and said, "Craig and Barbara used to be smugglers and have all kinds of connections throughout the galaxy. They might know something."

"We should let the Department of Homeworld Security know as well," Marq said.

Kral's grip on Becca's shoulder tightened. Did that mean he wanted them involved or wanted them kept out of it?

"What can they do?" Becca asked. "Aren't they all just Earthlings?"

"Brendan is one of the most intelligent sentients I've ever met," Marq said. "Just don't tell him I said that. And Sarah is the liaison to the Vegans. She can reach out to them."

Everyone seemed to be pulling out the stops to help. The backs of Becca's eyes started to burn a bit.

"Thanks," she said.

Marq nodded. "I'll also alert the Coalition's new leader, General Serath. If they've taken Sophie out of the Sol system, we may need to transit through blue space to follow."

Becca hadn't thought of Sophie being taken that far away. She *couldn't* think of it. But now that Marq had said it, all she could think of was how big the universe was. How would they ever find Sophie in it?

"Will the Cygnians be able to assist with the search?" Marq asked.

"You have my prism and my ship," Kral said. "I can't promise more."

His statement felt like a slap in the face. Everyone else —and it really sounded like *everyone*—was getting involved in the search. But Kral's people were sitting it out?

Becca supposed it wasn't really their concern. It was

weirder that so many people cared about one human. She should consider herself lucky that they did.

But with how Kral and the others had spoken about the Coalition earlier and from what Becca had now seen with her own eyes, she was having trouble understanding why Marq and Vay's people were so ready to help and Kral's people weren't. She had really expected more from them.

More from *him*.

Becca turned to Kral and said, "Can I talk to you for a minute? Privately?"

"We'll work with them," Lar said.

Kral nodded. He took her hand in his and led Becca to a small room off to the side of the hangar bay. The walls were a mix of glass, or something else that was transparent, and some smooth white material that looked like metal or maybe plastic. Very sci-fi spaceship chic.

He closed the door behind them.

Becca looked out the window at the group of people— aliens—comparing notes. Notes that might determine if her sister…

She shook her head, unwilling to even consider the possibility.

"So much for privacy," she said.

"This is as good as we'll get for the moment. No one can hear us. What is it you needed to say?"

She stepped in close, her arms crossed. "Whoever is behind this wants to drive a wedge between Sadirians and

Cygnians. Whether it's rogue Coalition people or the Assembly."

"I agree," Kral said.

"Are you going to let them win? Give them what they want?"

His lips curled back in a snarl. Yeah, she didn't think he'd like that.

"They're trying to manipulate your people," she said. "And if you sit on the sidelines, you're sending them the message that it's working."

"There are factors involved that you aren't aware of," Kral said.

"Then educate me."

"My parents don't support our alliance with Earth. They haven't come out against it yet, but that's probably because they thought we would grow bored with the planet and move on."

"Bored," she said.

"My prism and I don't usually spend this much time in one place when we're outside of Cygnian space."

"Then why Earth?"

He was quiet for a moment, then let out a sigh. "We have reason to believe that Cygnians are biologically compatible with Earthlings."

"So?"

"This doesn't surprise you?"

"Nuar told me."

His eyebrows arched. "Why would he do that?"

Becca felt her cheeks heat, but she just funneled that into her glare. "Because I asked him." She hurried on before Kral's enigmatic smirk could derail her train of thought. "And I know about your population problem, too. What I don't get is why your people wouldn't be climbing all over themselves to help us out and get on good terms with us."

"Because we are also compatible with Sadirians. My parents are more interested in securing an alliance with the Coalition."

That stung. Her planet had its problems, but still.

"I don't get why they would choose Sadirians over Earthlings," she said.

"Sadirians are aware of alien life. They have advanced technology. There would be less culture-shock for them to navigate in bonding with us. I've only spoken with my father about it, but he was very clear in the direction he wants our people to take."

She did not like Kral talking about bonding with a Sadirian. And it bothered her that she was so bothered by it.

"Who died and made him king?" she said.

Kral opened his mouth, then closed it. He actually looked away, as if he couldn't bring himself to answer her.

"Kral." Becca reached out to him and clasped his wrists.

He turned to her, his eyes glowing with that orange light. Electric currents ran up her arms, joining with the pulse racing up and down her spine. Heat exploded in her core and her skin felt electrified.

Kral stepped closer, lifting a hand to run his fingers through her hair, brushing it from her face. She swore she felt the air around them vibrating.

She thought again of what Nuar had said about the soulmate bond and achieving frequency. How it was unmistakable. And how they could bond with Earthlings.

Could Kral be the other half of her soul?

"My grandfather," Kral said, breaking her out of her thoughts.

Becca's brain kind of stalled. What had they been talking about? "I'm sorry, what now?"

"You asked…"

He hesitated again. What could this huge warrior be so reluctant to say?

"My grandfather, Keril," Kral said. "When he died, the title of king passed on to my father."

"King," she repeated. Her thoughts were spinning in circles. "But that would make you…"

"Crown prince. Heir to the throne of Cygnus-Prime."

"You're a prince." She paused a moment, then turned around and walked a few paces away, fighting the pull that made her want to stay right next to him.

"Becca, are you all right?"

No, she was not all right.

Her sister was missing. She was on a warship in outer space. Amy was stuck in a crystal stasis chamber for who knew how long. Aliens were real and the ones she'd met so far were disappointingly mundane.

Except for Kral. Who might be her soulmate, no matter how much she wanted to not believe it.

But Kral was a prince. *The* prince for his people.

A space prince.

Was this the piece that was finally going to push her over the edge into "absolutely not able to handle this" territory? She took a deep breath and blew it out.

No, that wasn't what was making her think that she might let out a scream from it all.

What bothered her was that his parents didn't approve of Earthlings.

They would rather see Kral married to some Sadirian woman, even with the creepy-as-hell stuff they'd done to their people. And if his parents felt that way, Becca would bet more of Kral's people were just as averse to him becoming involved with her.

She was just a backwoods bumpkin to the Cygnians. There was no way they'd accept her being with Kral. Not if he was their prince.

Why the hell did she even care? She'd only just met the guy. All this soulmate talk was bullshit.

And yet, the thought of Kral with another woman had

Becca ready to try to find something to chuck through the big window between them and the hangar bay. Maybe she'd throw Kral. It might knock some sense into him.

Did he agree with his parents? It was hard to believe, with the way he looked at her and that incredible near-kiss moment they'd shared.

Now, she wasn't sure she'd ever get a chance like that again. She wasn't interested in being some kind of fling— something to stave off the boredom of being the royal heir to a freaking planetary system. One with its own black hole, no less.

This wasn't right. They didn't even know her. They didn't know Earth.

She ground her teeth together so hard her jaw started to hurt.

If Kral's people thought she didn't deserve him—that no one from Earth deserved a chance—then they could all go straight to hell.

Kral had said his parents were waiting for him to get bored. Was that who Kral was?

If it was true, once he grew bored, Kral would leave. Just like all the other guys she'd dated.

I guess he doesn't just look like a normal guy. He's exactly like them, through and through.

"Fine, then," she said. "If King Dad doesn't approve of Earthlings, I can ask Nika for help. That Marq guy seems eager to assist, and he's got all kinds of connections that

—"

"I have pledged to help you," Kral said. "We won't turn our back on you or your sisters."

"Pledged to help. Is that why you're doing this? Because you feel like you made a promise? Well, let me un-make it for you. I release you from your pledge. Go off and do whatever you want to do to entertain yourselves."

"Becca—" He reached for her, but she jerked away.

She stormed toward the door, stopping when she reached it. There was no doorknob. No button. No keyhole or latch.

"How the fuck do I get out of this stupid room?" she said.

His hands brushed her shoulders. She turned around and shoved at him, but he didn't budge. Falling back into a fighting stance, she lifted her fists.

Kral's lips pulled back from his teeth, sending shivers all over her skin. His shoulders arched and his eyes crackled with heat.

"You should know before you challenge me that my people mate through combat," he said.

"You *fight* when you have sex?" She was not okay with that.

"What?" Some of the fire left his gaze. "No, of course not. We win the right to lifemates through combat. One challenges the other, and through victory, they are wed."

"I'm not asking you to marry me, I just want you to

open the damn door!"

Kral's shoulders lowered. Was it her imagination, or did he look a little disappointed?

He reached past her and traced a pattern next to the door. It whooshed open. He opened his palm and gestured for her to exit first.

She paused in the doorway. "Out of curiosity and just so I'm sure I understand, does that mean that if someone wants to marry you, they have to beat you in combat?"

"If they issue the challenge, yes."

She shook her head. "I'm betting you're really good in a fight."

He cast the most feral smile at her she'd ever seen. "I am the best."

How could she feel even more despair in the middle of this crapstorm? And why was she even thinking about… marriage-fighting or whatever?

The pull she felt toward Kral was part of what was keeping her moving forward. There were moments when she felt like it was the *only* thing that was keeping her moving forward. To know that in the end it couldn't go anywhere…

"Cygnians seem stubborn," she said. "Do you ever change?"

"I want us to. We need to find compromises."

As ridiculous as it was, she wondered if any of those compromises might make a way to a future for them. Or if he even wanted them to.

But she had more urgent things she needed to focus on.

"Right now, I need to find my sister," she said.

Kral nodded, then followed her from the room.

Chapter Fourteen

"We think we have something." Vay's tone betrayed her excitement.

Kral quickened his pace to match Becca's as she practically ran to the group clustered outside of the *Arrow*. They had moved to the far wall of the hangar bay, where they could access a vidscreen.

"So soon?" Kral said.

"It seems Vay's Lyrian connections deserve their reputation," Lar said.

"Craig and Barbara aren't actively smuggling right now, but Hank—their son—is," Vay said. "We think most of the aliens who were trespassing on Earth left shortly after the Vegans arrived. Apparently there are facilities in the asteroid field between Mars and Jupiter that were used as a base of operations for them."

"And Hank thinks they might still be in use?" Kral asked.

"He does," Vay said. "And it gets better."

"One of the bases that is believed to still be in use belongs to the Tau Ceti," Lar said.

"That is fortunate," Kral said.

"But our luck ends there." Marq tapped on a control next to the vidscreen. It filled with a view of asteroids floating against the backdrop of space. "Even if the *Reckoning* could navigate such a dense asteroid field, the ship doesn't have a cloaking field."

"A ship this size could easily generate a cloaking field." Kral was surprised both at the oversight and the fact that Marq would share such a weakness so easily.

"The High Council wanted their warships to be seen," Marq said. "To create fear and obedience among our citizens. They didn't see the need for a cloaking field. We're looking into retrofitting both the *Reckoning* and the *Arbiter* with the devices, but it will take some time to get them in place. We're being masked by Vegan cloaking generators at the moment."

Yet more intelligence that could work against his people if the Cygnians decided to side with the Assembly at some point.

"I appreciate your candor," Kral said.

"We need to share our resources if we're going to rescue Sophie," Marq said. "The longer they have her, the more chances they'll move her out of the system."

"And that's bad, right?" A deep furrow rested between Becca's brows and her skin had paled.

"It's a big universe," Marq said.

"And one that Sophie will see from the heart of a Cygnian vessel, not some Tau Ceti ship," Lar practically snarled the words.

Kral wondered where Lar's usual calm had fled to. Lar was the best at dealing with delicate situations and controlling his emotions. It was why he was in charge of communications.

He would ask about it later. Kral needed to keep his focus on finding Sophie.

"The *Arrow* will enter the asteroid field and scan for facilities," Kral said.

"We'll provide you with everything we have about the bases," Marq said. "And we'll be standing by to provide support as needed."

Vay cleared her throat and stood a little straighter. "You should know we've notified Buddy. Well, I notified him. He needed to know."

Kral nodded. "It was the right thing to do. I only wish I had been the one to tell him."

"Oh, I think it was better coming from me," Vay said. She half-cringed and shrugged. "He was really mad."

"All the more reason I should have been the one to receive his ire." Kral had always thought Buddy's desire to keep his family away from his alien activities was strange and unnecessary. But after this, he understood Buddy's concern.

Becca's sisters had been attacked within hours of Kral approaching them. The timing couldn't be a coincidence.

But why would they wait until that moment to make

their move? Why not make it sooner?

"If we have everything we need, we should go, right?" Becca said, looking around at the faces surrounding her.

"Yes." Marq deactivated the vidscreen. "The asteroid field is large. It could take days of scanning to find the facility you're looking for."

"Days?" Becca said.

Kral put his hand on her shoulder. Tendrils of energy unwound, moving up his arm.

He could feel her fear. Her unrest.

She wanted to do something. She needed something to fight.

It was a sentiment they shared.

"They're going to have her for days," Becca whispered. She closed her eyes and shook her head, then wheeled around and wrapped her arms around Kral's waist, burying her face against his chest.

He felt his eyes widen, but then held her as the others looked on. The members of his prism moved closer, each warrior placing a hand on Becca's back.

"We will find her," Lar said. "That, I promise you."

"And it won't take us days," Dorn added.

Bron glanced over his shoulder at the Sadirians. "Our scanners are more powerful than what the Coalition uses. We can see through much denser objects."

"Just remember not to fry anything you're trying to scan," Vay said. "Earthlings are as fragile as Sadirians and we don't know who or what else is being held with Sophie."

Becca's grip on Kral tightened. He smoothed down her hair.

"We will hunt them," Kral said. "We will find them. And we will make them pay for what they've done."

Becca trembled. He felt her take in a deep breath, then she stepped back.

Her eyes shone with a fierce light. She nodded once, then glanced at the warriors surrounding her.

"Then let's get moving." She marched toward the ship. Dorn, Lar, and Bron fell in step right behind her without hesitating.

She was a natural leader. Strong and brave. If his people—or his parents—couldn't see that... Well, Kral would have some hard conversations ahead of him.

He would not walk away from Becca. Never again.

"Kral." Vay grabbed his elbow as he turned to follow the group. She dropped her voice to barely above a whisper. "You and Becca seem to be...getting along well."

"And?" Kral let the word drip with warning.

"Buddy told me he noticed something between you," Vay said. "I think it's pretty obvious to anyone who sees you together."

"If you have a point to make, Vay, make it," Kral said.

"I thought Becca was Sophie when I first saw her," Vay said. "All we had were vids and Earth pictures to go on.

Have you thought that maybe the Tau Ceti weren't just going after Buddy's sisters to upset your prism?"

Kral's spine plates quivered and began to rise.

"When you left Harbor, you left the Vegan security measures we have in place for counter-surveillance," Vay said. "I mean, it would be one thing if they just wanted to mess with your friend's family. But if they had an agent watching you, and they saw you with Becca and noticed this…energy between you—"

"You think they were after Becca and took Sophie instead by accident." Kral's voice was a low rumble that made the floor beneath them tremble. His spine plates stuck out from his back, adding their thrumming power to the vibration. "You think they know that she's mine and want to take her from me."

"Vay." Marq had been giving them space, but he stepped closer, grabbing Vay's arm and pulling her away from Kral.

Kral lifted a hand in a gesture of peace, noting without surprise the claws that had extended from his fingers. He took a deep breath and forced his spine plates to lower.

How obvious was his attraction to Becca?

Vay had given him his answer. As had the other warriors in how they had placed themselves in her service, gathering to support her, following when she gave the order to leave.

They were already treating her as their someday queen.

If the Coalition's enemies had seen Becca and Kral together—and he'd given them ample opportunity to do so —they would know how he felt. They would know what she meant to him.

They would know what she was worth.

"I will consider your words." Kral turned and stalked toward his ship.

Most of the others had gone aboard, but Dorn waited for him.

"Did you hear?" Kral asked as they scaled the ramp.

"Yes."

"Did Becca?"

"No," Dorn said.

The moment they reached the top of the ramp, Dorn pressed the control to retract it and seal the hatch.

Kral hesitated a moment. "Did she see?"

"Your spine rising in challenge? No."

Kral let out a long breath.

"She hasn't seen you," Dorn said.

Kral shook his head.

"Why?" Dorn asked.

"Because, for once in my life, I'm afraid. I don't know how she'll react."

"If she is to be our queen, she must accept us as we are. If she can't, then she isn't your soulmate."

He said it as if it was such a simple thing, and not as though Kral's hearts hung in the balance.

Kral followed the sound of voices to the common room. Becca wasn't there.

"She went to check on Amy," Lar said. He was sitting on a bench built into the wall. Dash rested next to him, her head resting on his leg as he scratched behind her ear.

"How is Amy?" Kral asked.

"She needs a full Earth week in the healing chamber," Lar said.

Only the worst injuries would require that much time to heal. She must have come so close to death.

And Kral had brought this on her.

"Rom is piloting us out of the *Reckoning*," Bron said. "And I've received the data I'll need to set up my scans. Tarn is on his way up from engineering to assist me."

Kral nodded.

"Buddy warned us to stay away," Kral said. "But we didn't. Now, enemies we didn't even know we had have moved against us."

"Coalition politics—" Bron began.

"They were after Becca," Kral shouted. "Because they know what my parents will not recognize."

Kral's lips peeled back from his teeth and his claws descended. The plates of his spine shivered into place, finally tearing through his thin Earth shirt. He let out a disgusted grunt and pulled the fabric away from his body, throwing it to the floor.

"There is no more 'Coalition politics' or 'Cygnian

politics,'" he said. "There is only our enemies and the battles to be fought. When we can prove the Assembly is behind this, we will go to war and we will obliterate them and anyone else who stands in our way."

Each warrior stood and struck their wristbands together, the sound reverberating through the room. They stomped their feet in unison, signifying their readiness to follow him into battle.

"And our Cygnian brothers will recognize our connection with Earth, whether they want to or not," Kral continued. "My father is right. To survive, we must change our ways. But we will stand with Earth. Becca is my soulmate. I'm sure of it. And this attack on her is an attack on our hearts. It will not be allowed to pass without bloody retribution."

They struck their wristbands together again.

Lar's eyes widened, and he lowered his arms. The other men did the same.

That was not what Kral had expected.

"Are you not behind me in this?" Kral asked.

"Of course we are." Lar lifted a hand. "But…Becca is behind you as well."

Behind him. As in, she could see his back and the quivering spine plates standing up along its length.

He spun around, as if that could make her un-see what she had seen.

Her eyes were wide and her mouth hung open. Her

gaze locked on his.

At that moment, Tarn strode into the common room.

Without his holo-emitter on.

He paused as every face turned to him.

Kral's hearts pounded against his sides. He didn't dare to move.

Would Becca be afraid of him? Revolted at his alien appearance?

She hadn't even started out seeing Kral's true coloration. That would have been so much better than her seeing his body ready for battle.

Now, she was staring at Tarn, her eyes wide enough that Kral could see the whites all around them. What must she be thinking?

Tarn's short hair was a livid blue that matched his skin. The bright indigo of his eyes stood out in a contrast so strong, it was difficult for most non-Cygnians to hold his gaze. He wore his Cygnian leathers, the white tunic leaving his arms and much of his lithe chest bare.

Tarn paused, taking in all the stares, then he smiled. "I'm going to assume that my timing is absolutely impeccable, as always, and that all this attention is due to you being awestruck at my perfect entrance."

"We're supposed to have our holo-emitters active while there's an Earthling on the ship," Lar said.

Tarn scoffed. "This is my home and this is me. I won't hide what I am."

"Tarn—" Lar began.

Becca cleared her throat. "Holo-emitters? Somebody mentioned those before. I meant to ask." She looked around the room, stopping on Kral. "So, you're all blue? Or are you different colors under there?"

Dorn lifted his arms and clanged his wristbands together, humming the sound that deactivated his holo-emitter. Becca gasped as his skin turned to a pale blue, his hair almost white.

Bron went next, his deep blue the color of Earth's skies at midnight, and his hair even darker.

She looked at Lar, her mouth closed and eyes narrowed now. He bowed his head, then deactivated his holo-emitter, revealing his cobalt blue skin and shimmering blue hair.

Finally, Becca turned to Kral. She crossed her arms over her chest and glared at him. He didn't know if that was a good sign or not, but was somewhat encouraged.

Kral lifted his arms slowly, then clanged his wristbands together, humming the sound that deactivated his holo-emitter. With his shirt gone, Becca could see all of his cerulean skin and his sapphire-blue hair.

She stared at him for a very long time, not saying anything. Finally, she said, "When were you going to tell me?"

"This is who we are," Kral said. "Why should it matter if our appearances are different than yours?"

"I don't give a shit that you're blue," she said. "Or

spiny with claws or even that you're the space prince of some black-hole planet system." She took a menacing step forward and said, "When were you going to tell me that I'm your soulmate?"

Chapter Fifteen

Becca's heart was pounding as Kral stared into her eyes. He broke the silence after a few moments.

"Bron and Tarn, continue your work calibrating our scans and let Rom know the route he needs to take," Kral said. "Lar and Dorn, create a plan for infiltrating their base and bringing Sophie out safely."

He was good at dishing out orders. Becca would give him that. But she wasn't going to be bossed around or left in the dark.

Becca arched her eyebrows at him. "And?"

"And Becca..." Kral paused for a few moments, then said "Let's go somewhere that we can talk. Privately."

He gestured toward one of the passages that she hadn't been down yet.

"Oh, no," she said. "After you."

She thought she heard one of the other men let out a muffled laugh, but didn't dare look away from Kral. His eyes flared bright orange as he held her gaze.

Finally, he turned and headed down the hallway. She uncrossed her arms and followed him, trying to act as if her heart wasn't about to jump out of her chest.

Kral was her soulmate. At least, he thought he was. Given her reaction to him, she could easily believe it.

Excitement warred with nerves.

Kral wasn't just an alien. He was the crown prince of his planet. If Becca was his soulmate, what did that make her?

She'd never been one to play princess. The idea of becoming one was not appealing, although, with the whole warrior thing they had going on, maybe she'd be okay with it.

But even if she was his soulmate, would his people accept her? Did she want them to?

She studied Kral as he walked in front of her. Damn, he had an amazing back. And arms. And...entire body.

She loved seeing him without his shirt on. It made her want to touch him—to explore their similarities and their obvious differences.

Kral's spine was covered in midnight-blue ovals that ran down the middle of his back. An even darker line ran the length of them, slightly raised from the ovals.

She'd seen serrated spines coming out of them earlier, kind of like the plates on a stegosaurus. They had been blurred a bit, as if they were moving too fast for her to see. She could feel waves of vibration rippling out in the air around them.

He also had claws at the ends of his fingers. They had to be retractable, or she would have noticed them earlier.

And, of course, there were those sharp teeth.

She found herself wondering what else was different about him. And was this really her soulmate?

She couldn't deny that she felt a pull to him. A bond that went beyond the physical need to be close. Now that she was seeing him without his holo-emitter, that need was taking on all kinds of new meaning.

Until now, the aliens she had met had seemed so... mundane. They all looked just like humans. Or at least, that's what she'd thought.

She wished that she had been able to see Kral as he truly was right from the beginning. That would have made for an interesting family dinner. Everyone would have had a million questions, starting with her mom grilling him on whether he could eat Buddy's food safely and if he needed anything to be more comfortable.

Her family would welcome Kral and the others in his prism. Why had Buddy felt the need to keep this secret?

Okay, he probably had known Sophie would ogle them all, holo-emitters or not. Not that Becca had room to talk. She was practically drooling over the muscles of Kral's back as he walked in front of her.

She wanted him—wanted to explore more of whatever this was that they had. Whether his people accepted her or not, in this moment, she needed to know what *Kral* wanted.

He placed his hand on a panel next to a doorway and it

slid open. Again, he gestured for her to go first. This time, she accepted his offer.

She stepped into a large bedroom. Yup, a bedroom.

Oh boy.

A huge bed dominated one side of the room, covered in blankets and pillows. The other side of the room was partitioned off, but through the semi-transparent walls, she could see a chair and a desk that seemed to be built into the wall.

Of course, Kral led her to the bed.

Her mind started playing through vivid fantasies of what could come next. Her hands splayed over his chest, exploring all those muscles and the ridges along his spine. She could bury her hands in his mane of hair, finally learn what his kiss was like.

She walked to the bed and sat down on the edge of it, sinking into the piles of blankets. Beneath that was the hardest mattress she had ever felt. She lifted the edge of the blankets to look at it.

The bed looked like it was made of the same milky white material as the ship.

"No way," she said. "Do you honestly sleep on that?"

He let out a low, rumbling chuckle that made her want to curl her toes.

"All Cygnians do," he said. "Almost everything on our planet is made up of crystals and rocks. When Vay and Buddy introduced us to Earth bedding, we thought it was a joke. Bron says he feels like he's sinking into the ground when he lies on them, and refuses to go near regular mattresses because he's afraid of suffocating." Kral cringed a bit. "But don't tell him I told you that."

Becca could imagine the huge warrior slowly sinking into a mattress, his eyes growing wider with panic as it started to swallow him up.

"No worries," she said. "And I totally get it."

"The rest of us have a contest going on to see who can stand the softest bed. We sneak extra blankets and pillows into each others' rooms and see how long it takes for the complaints to start."

She let out a laugh. That seemed like the kind of thing she and her siblings would do to each other.

"Well, I'm glad you have that little prank-contest going," she said. "I don't like the idea of sitting on a rock while we look for Sophie."

"We'll find her," Kral said.

"But will we find her in time?"

He knelt in front of her and held her hands in his. Damn, he was tall. Even on his knees, they were on eye level as she sat.

"We will rescue her," he said. "I have no doubt of it."

"How can you be sure?"

"Because the universe led me to you. It wouldn't be so cruel as to begin our...friendship...with such a hardship."

"Friendship, huh?" She arched an eyebrow. "I thought

we were soulmates?"

His lips parted, but instead of speaking, he lifted her hands to his lips for a gentle kiss.

Gentle or not, it sent fire raging through her body. The idea of those huge hands on her body, those firm lips exploring hers...

She wanted to reach out and grab him and kiss him until they both forgot about everything else going on.

"I don't believe in soulmates," she said, pulling her hands from his grasp.

He surprised her by nodding. "From what I know of your culture, I understand that. Nonetheless, among the Cygnians, the existence of soulmates is a given. Too many of us have first hand experience with it."

"Like with your prism?"

He nodded again. "Lar is from the same region as my mother. We were visiting her relatives when I met him in one of the crystal woods."

Crystal woods? She made a mental note to ask Kral about that later. She'd love to know what those looked like.

"I was a spoiled child with a wild temper," Kral said. "I wanted to break off one of the branches of the tree to give as a gift to my mother. Lar was the self-appointed guardian of the forest."

"I take it your first meeting didn't go well?"

Kral laughed. "It went perfectly. Just as the universe

wanted it to. Lar had no idea who I was, and I don't think he would have cared even if I'd told him. We also didn't know what it meant to be part of a prism yet. We fought, our movements synchronized to the point that we knew something was going on."

"And you realized you were destined to be besties."

Again, he laughed. "Actually, we ended up smashing into one of the trees, causing shards of crystal to rain down on us. I shoved Lar out of the way of a branch that would have skewered him, but..."

He lifted his right arm, revealing a long scar that ran down the back of his bicep. "Our skin hardens as we age. Not many Cygnians have scars. But I was foolish. I didn't make it clear of the rest of the falling debris. Lar grabbed one of the broken branches and stood over me, knocking the shards aside as they rained down. Our parents had the branch honed into a crystal blade that he carries into battle to this day. No one can match his skill with the sword."

"No wonder you two are so close. You saved each other's lives. But that doesn't mean there's some kind of psychic connection."

"We felt the connection before we fought and during. Our bond has only grown stronger as we've experienced life together, as it has for everyone in our prism."

"How does a soulmate even fit in with that?" She was mostly talking to herself, but she really did want to know the answer. "If these men are so important to you—"

"Nothing is more important to me than you," Kral said. "And they all know and understand that. Envy it, even."

She wanted to believe him. She was just so used to being disappointed. So far, Kral hadn't actually let her down. Would he eventually?

"We just met," she said. "You don't even know me."

"I know what I feel for you," he said.

She reached out tentatively, resting her hands above his heart. Well, where it would have been if he'd been human.

His chest was warm and solid. As hard as a rock, but smooth to the touch.

He smirked at her, then grasped her hands again, moving them to the sides of his chest and pressing them against his ribs near his arms.

Strong beats drummed beneath her fingers. She gasped and looked up at him.

"My hearts came close to beating in unison for the first time when I heard you sing," Kral said. "They do the same any time you're close to me—but only then."

Becca swallowed past a lump in her throat. The beat thrummed up her arms, only slightly off from each other.

She could feel her own heartbeat in her ears, the cadence matching Kral's almost perfectly. As she listened, she couldn't tell whose heart she felt.

The sound and feeling merged together, pulling her closer to Kral. She felt as if his arms were around her, even though he hadn't moved—a sense of safety and belonging that went beyond anything she'd experienced before.

He felt like home.

Kral released one of her hands, but there was no way she could move away, even if she wanted to. He placed his palm on her sternum, his hand so large that his fingers curled up over her collarbone.

"I feel you in me," Kral said. "In my hearts, in my soul. You are the only one in this universe who can make me feel this complete."

"We..." Her mouth had gone dry, and she struggled to whisper the words. "We don't even know each other."

"I know that you are brave enough to follow this mission through, no matter where it takes you. That you love your family enough that you will never back down when it comes to protecting them. I know that you refuse to tolerate those who would disrespect you or others, and you aren't afraid to follow through on your beliefs with action. I know that you aren't intimidated by an entire prism of the greatest Cygnian Warriors in the universe. And I know that I will love you more with each passing day for the rest of my life."

Her heart beat faster. Kral's followed. She wanted to believe him. Wanted to believe all of this. But it seemed too good to be true. And when something seemed too good to be true...

She shook her head.

"What do you need to know of me that your heart can't tell you?" Kral asked, his voice painfully gentle.

What *did* she need to know?

He loved his friends like family. He loved Buddy and he loved dogs—especially Pickles. Kral had had her back at the shop when those jerks were giving her a hard time, but had given her space to take care of it herself instead of trying to rescue her.

He got along with her sisters and was now defying his parents—his king and queen—to help them. To help *her*.

He respected her, yet stood up for himself when they disagreed. That was something she'd rarely encountered with past boyfriends. Either they would go all macho on her and try to bully her into agreeing with them or they'd sulk and be passive-aggressive later.

She couldn't imagine Kral ever being passive. Supportive, yes. Maintaining a calculated distance, sure. But when he knew what he wanted, he went for it.

And he wanted *her*.

She wanted him, too.

"What does your heart tell you, Becca?" he murmured, his voice a low rumble that went straight to her core.

"That I've been waiting for you my whole life."

Desire flared in his eyes and his lips twitched up in a near-snarl.

Then they were on her—*he* was on her—pushing her back onto the bed.

His lips crashed down onto hers, firm and warm and demanding. She buried her fingers in his hair, keeping him close.

With one hand, he grabbed her backside, lifting her entire body into the air as he moved them further up onto the bed. She held onto his shoulders as he laid her back down, nestling between her legs.

Sparks were already unfurling from her core, traveling along her nerves and making her almost ravenous with need. She wrapped her legs around the backs of his thighs, encouraging him as he thrust against her through their clothes.

He was so hard—everywhere. Especially the long, thick cock she could feel pressing against her.

She ran her hands down his back, exploring the plates that ran along his spine, all of them now fully erect. He released her lips as she did, pinning her to the bed harder with his hips as he let out a feral growl.

"Becca," he groaned.

So, that was a spot she was going to remember. There had to be other places she could find that would drive him wild.

He rolled off of her, all the way across the large bed, and came up in a crouch. His eyes were molten lava, illuminating strong cheekbones and casting shadows across his brow.

She lifted herself onto her elbows, wondering if she'd

done something wrong.

"Naked," he grunted. "Now. Or I will tear off your clothes with my teeth."

He snarled, showing he could make good on his words.

The thought of him ripping her clothes to shreds sent waves of goosebumps all over her body. But she didn't have any to spare.

She rolled the other direction, way less gracefully than he had probably, and sprang to her feet. As quickly as she could, she pulled off her tank top, kicked off her shoes, and shimmied out of her jeans. She already wasn't wearing a bra, and she did away with her panties and socks before turning back around.

"Oh... shit..." she said.

Kral had made good use of his time. He was standing on the other side of the bed completely naked.

The light from the chamber rippled across his deep blue skin in waves of silver as he moved. He was corded with thick muscle everywhere. Thighs like tree-trunks, massive arms, pecs that made her drool, and rows of abdominal muscles—more than a six pack, as she'd noted earlier.

Her eyes locked onto his cock, and she was relieved to see that it looked...compatible. If she could manage it, anyway.

She did a double-take as she realized there were two of them. Two cocks.

Oh my God...

Kral leapt up onto the bed and crouched in its center. She had half expected him to leap at her and plow into her. If she thought she could manage him, she wouldn't even mind.

Instead, he dropped to his knees.

"Come to me," he said. "Now."

She wanted to light into him with some quip about him not being the boss of her, but at the moment, all she could think about was having him buried deep inside of her. She'd kick his ass for that comment later.

Then again, maybe she could arrange to give him a little punishment sooner.

On all fours, she crawled across the bed toward him. As she drew close, she could hear a low growl vibrating in his chest. She could even feel it through the "mattress" beneath her.

His fingers flexed and curled, as if he couldn't wait to grab her.

But she was going to make him.

"Don't touch me," she said.

Surprise flashed across his features, as well as a wave of disappointment. She couldn't let that last.

"Until I say so," she added.

His gaze settled back into an intense stare. "You have my word."

"Good. Because I intend to test your Cygnian mettle."

Chapter Sixteen

Kral was going to burst from his skin. His blood rushed through his veins with each powerful beat of his hearts, filling him with strength. He felt as though he could claw through the walls of the ship, rip the crystal of his bed to pieces, drive himself into Becca over and over until their eternity claimed them.

His cocks throbbed, longing to be buried within her. He wanted her with a need that terrified him.

But he had to be careful. One wrong move, and he could hurt her.

Nuar had given Lian his wristbands when they had bonded. They could generate shielding that would protect Becca and yet not diminish their time together.

Kral struck his wristbands together to activate them. He hummed the note to release them from his wrists, then offered them to Becca.

"You need to put these on before we go any further," he said.

Becca arched an eyebrow. "I'm not into jewelry."

"These aren't just jewelry. They control much of our technology and can generate shielding that will protect you."

"From what?"

"From me."

He had wondered if he might see a flicker of fear at that. Her expression grew serious, but she nodded and took the wristbands. Once she placed them over her arms, they shrank to fit her perfectly.

"That's handy," she said.

Kral hummed the note that would activate the shielding. She gave a little gasp as the pale gold light flickered over her, only visible for a moment.

"I'll still feel you through this?" she asked.

"As if it isn't there. But if I get carried away, it will keep you from being injured."

"Good plan. What about kids?"

His hearts stuttered at her question, the thought of giving her children causing his throat to close painfully with the weight of his disappointment.

"I can only give you children if we work with scientists to make it so," Kral said. "I... I'm sorry."

Surprise flashed across her features. "I was only asking if it would kind of act as a contraceptive," she said. "We don't have to worry about kids for a long time."

"I want children." He could hear the desperate note in his own voice and didn't care.

Becca smiled. "Me, too. But let's learn to enjoy each other first. Deal?"

He smiled back. "Deal."

"So, where were we?"

"I believe you had issued a challenge," Kral said. "Your plan to test my Cygnian mettle?"

"Nice to know you're paying attention."

She grinned, then lowered herself in front of him on all fours. Kral was confused. There wasn't much she could do from there to test him.

He wanted her on her back beneath him, but having her between the hard bed and his body wouldn't be safe. He would have to pull her on top of him to take her as—

His thoughts screeched to a halt as she opened her mouth and wrapped her lips around his primary cock. He let out a guttural shout as bolts of pleasure tore through his body. Her tongue flicked over his crown and another blast of sensation had him almost doubling over.

Then her lips were wrapped around him, sucking hard as she slid her head up and down his shaft, taking what little of him she could into her mouth and wrapping one hand around more of him. With her other hand, she stroked the secondary cock beneath it, running her fingertips over its ridges. She squeezed him hard, her hands moving in concert with her mouth, her tongue pressed to his shaft, swirling and pulling.

He couldn't breathe. The pressure in his chest built as his hearts continued their near-unified beat. His hands reached for her, wanting to touch the smooth skin of her back, to squeeze her ass, to grip her hair to better feel the movement of her mouth on him.

As if she sensed his thoughts, she pulled herself back, letting him slide from her mouth, and said, "No touching."

Kral snarled. His lips peeled back from his teeth. He curled his hands into fists, his claws digging against his palms.

She drew him into her mouth again.

How could pleasure also be agony?

She alternated her strokes, bringing him so close to the edge of blistering ecstasy that the edges of his vision turned white, then slowing to a tortuous pace that let him feel every flick and swirl of her tongue.

He put his hands on the back of his head to keep from grabbing her, his chest heaving with his breaths.

"Becca," he groaned, surprised at the pleading note to his voice.

She pulled back and rose on her knees, raking her fingernails across his chest. After feeling so much of her attention centered on his cocks, that little touch sent his nerves into freefall.

He wanted to grab her, to throw her on her stomach, lift her hips to his, and drive into her.

But he'd given his word, and she hadn't granted permission. When would she let him touch her?

"Stay just like that," Becca said, sitting back on her heels and spreading her knees apart. She ran a finger along his cocks, making them jerk.

He kept his hands on his head, fingers grabbing fistfuls of his hair to vent some of his frustration.

Her gaze roved greedily over his body. "You are the most beautiful man I've ever seen. And I need to get ready for you."

"Ready?" He was panting as he spoke. "How?"

She looked at him and smirked. That hand near his cocks wrapped around his primary shaft again, holding tight. The other...

She slid her hand down her stomach and through the short curls between her legs. Her eyes darkened and she gasped, running her fingers along the folds of her skin. As he watched, she slid two of her fingers deep into her core.

Keepers of Light, was this how Earthlings had sex? Kral wasn't sure he'd survive it.

"I'm so wet for you," she said. "I can't wait to feel you buried deep inside me."

Becca rose up on her knees, slowly running her other hand along the cock she held. She matched the movement with what she was doing to herself, flexing her fingers and bringing them to the apex of her slit repeatedly.

"Nor can I."

"Nuar said we're physiologically compatible," she said.

Kral snarled at her mentioning another male while they were sharing this.

"Settle down." Her tone was placating, and she gave

his cock a squeeze. "What about pleasure? You seem to react well to what I'm doing. Do you know what pleases me?"

"I vow to spend the rest of my lifetime learning every way to make you scream in ecstasy," he said.

She grinned. "I'm more interested in right now. You have these ridges." She ran her fingertips along the bottom of his primary cock. "And this..."

She traced the backs of her fingers against the most pronounced ridge, on the top of his cock near its base. Her voice hitched as she moved her fingers to the front of her slit again. "I'm guessing Cygnian women have a clitoris, too. If your bottom cock is riding me hard, this upper one will be sliding against me in all the right places."

He groaned at the picture she painted. He would take her with his smaller, secondary cock, preparing her body for true union. And then, he would drive his mating shaft into her. They would be bonded for eternity.

"I am fully equipped to pleasure you," he said. "If you will give me permission to do so."

Becca pulled her lower lip into her mouth, her teeth biting down as she swirled her fingertips against herself and squeezed his cock hard.

"Becca, please."

She smiled, a huntress's smile. Wild and triumphant.

"You may touch me now," she said.

Kral grabbed her arms the moment the words left her

lips. He pulled her against his chest and kissed her, his tongue delving deep.

She groaned, reaching around his sides as if she was going for his spine plates again.

He was barely holding it together as it was. He couldn't last if he let her touch him there. He was also too far gone to trust himself to throw her down and bury himself in her.

Instead, he wrapped his arms around her, pinning hers at her sides. He let his hands drift to her ass, cupping the slight mounds and squeezing. She groaned against his mouth.

He dropped to his side, bringing her with him and being careful not to crush any part of her. Rolling onto his back, he gripped her hips and pulled her on top of him, holding her above him easily. She braced herself against his chest.

It would be so easy to drive himself up into her. But it might cause her pain, and he couldn't risk that. Instead, he pushed her against his secondary cock, parting the incredibly soft folds of her slit.

She was so slick and wet. He pulled her along his length, angling her hips with his grip to ensure that he was hitting her clitoris with his movements. She groaned, digging her fingertips into his muscles and taking over the movement of her hips on her own.

Kral reached up to cup her breasts, flicking his thumbs across her taut nipples. She gasped, increasing the pace of her movement on him.

He reached down for her hips, lifting her so that her core was lined up with his crown. Slowly, he parted her tight flesh, barely nudging himself inside.

Her eyes clenched shut as she gasped in pleasure. His woman—his soulmate—so close to joining with him.

His spine plates wanted to rise, but his weight and the bed kept them in place. That plus the pleasure of Becca's hot, wet pussy was almost enough to make him lose control.

She had tortured him with denied pleasure earlier. He intended to repay her.

He pulled himself out, lifting her off of his shaft. She let out a little whimper and he smirked.

Again, he held her just above his cock, barely parting her flesh. He rotated his hips, his cock swirling at her opening, testing her readiness—and hopefully driving her as mad with lust as she'd done to him.

She groaned, her fingers clawing against his chest. His hearts were pounding, every instinct telling him to take her.

He pulled back again—this time, to slide her slit along his length. He ground against her clitoris until she was gasping, then lined her core up again with his cock barely parting her.

As he pulled her farther down, she wriggled her hips, desperately trying to take him in deeper. He held her steady, the gyration of her pussy on his crown nearly driving him mad with need.

She scowled, her eyes popping open so she could glare at him.

"Kral," she said.

He grinned at her and her scowl intensified—until he pressed himself deeper, just a bit.

She gasped, her eyes rolling shut again briefly. When she opened them again, she said, "Please."

He couldn't resist her plea. With a smooth thrust, he drove himself into her.

Heat and wetness assailed his senses. Becca cried out and threw her head back.

Kral kept his grip firm on her hips as he pounded into her, lifting her and pulling her down with each stroke. He could already feel her body throbbing around his shaft, another beat adding strength to the pulsing of their hearts.

He looked down to watch where they were joined, the blue of his thick shaft sliding in and out of her dark curls, her pale thighs clenched around his hips.

She leaned back, taking even more of him into her body, tightening the grip of her pussy on his cock. She reached behind herself and raked her nails along his thighs.

The sensation pushed him over the edge.

He pounded into her, hot jets of his seed pouring out of him, filling her, adding to her wetness. She let out a shriek of pure bliss that he added to with his own feral sounds. And always in the background was the cadence of their hearts.

As her body began to relax, he lifted her from him, his softening shaft sliding from her. In a fluid movement, he set her beside him then rose to his knees. He lifted her hips, lining up their bodies. With a swift movement, he drove his primary cock deep into her pussy.

She let out another scream, her core pulsing against him. Over and over, he pounded into her, his grip on her hips tight. She clawed at the sheets, crying out his name.

Her muscles bunched beneath him as she lifted herself up onto her knees, even as he kept driving into her. She reached up and wrapped her arms around his neck, pulling his face to hers for a kiss.

He drove his tongue into her, let his hands rove over her body. One cupped a breast, pinching and squeezing a taut nipple. The other went between her legs, his fingertips finding her wetness and swirling against her clitoris while he used his palm to keep her hips steady against his thrusts.

Everything he was coalesced into that space where they were joined, into the movement of her hips against his, the pulsing of her core, the pounding of his cock as he drew it in and out, faster and harder. He felt energy building, collapsing within himself, and then it exploded out through his body.

He threw his head back and let out a primal scream, Becca's voice joining his.

Light flooded his vision, rainbow patterns sparking across it. His ears were filled with the rushing sound of their breath, of the strong beat of their hearts—the single beat, his hearts achieving unity for the first time.

He could still feel her wrapped around his shaft, his cock buried as deep as it could be in her wet heat. His hands gripped her hips, her thighs pressed against his. She was holding onto his neck as tight as she could.

And more than that, he felt her excitement, her joy, her fear. Everything that she was—everything that they could be—spread across the horizon of his awareness.

He had never felt more complete and at peace.

As the light faded and the room slowly came back into view, rainbows hung in the air. Sparks of luminance danced around them.

"Am I hallucinating?" she said.

"You aren't."

"It's beautiful," she whispered.

He kissed the side of her neck. "It's unity."

He wanted to take her again. And again and again. They would never leave this chamber, if he could arrange it.

But he wanted even more than this with her. He wanted a life. A family. Adventures.

He wanted to show her the universe.

"How…" She turned to look at him with smoldering eyes and ran her fingertips across his cheek. "How can I already love you?"

Kral wanted to howl in triumph. To shout, "Victory!" so loud, they could hear it all through the ship, the Sol system, the galaxy itself.

Instead, he turned her to face him in his arms, holding her tight against his chest.

"Because," he said, "your heart has known me all along."

He leaned down and kissed her deeply, taking his time. His tongue explored, danced with hers.

They would have a lifetime of this. No one would stand in their way.

"Kral." Lar's voice sounded over the comm channel.

Kral let out a long growl. Becca joined in with him. He stopped at the unexpected sound. When their gazes locked, they both burst out laughing.

"Kral," Lar said again.

"This better be important." Kral's voice was another low growl.

"Yeah," Becca said, her voice low and raspy as well. Her eyes suddenly widened and she sat up straighter. "Did you find Sophie?"

"Not yet," Lar said. "But we're getting a priority transmission from Cygnus-Prime."

Kral sighed. "My father."

"Actually," Lar said, "the queen wishes to speak with you as well."

Chapter Seventeen

Becca walked next to Kral as they headed for the common room. He had her tucked into his side where she could feel the steady beat of one of his hearts.

She was so happy, she couldn't even worry about what Kral's parents were about to say or what they'd think of her. She and Kral would handle it. And they'd rescue Sophie and grind the people who had done this into powder beneath their feet.

His confidence was feeding into her. She could feel it.

She could really get used to this whole thinking like a Cygnian thing.

Maybe it was just the mind-blowing sex and sort of out-of-body experience after it. Everything had gone white, with rainbow patterns swirling through her vision. That was definitely a first.

Perks of finding her soulmate, she guessed.

The entire prism was waiting for them in the common room, standing around a man with long blue hair, a huge beard, and pale silver-blue skin. He was sitting behind a large desk that looked like it was made of a translucent blackish crystal. The chair he was sitting in looked like an enormous sapphire.

When the hell did they move that *in here?*

Behind him, a woman stood with her arms crossed over her chest. Her skin was cobalt blue, and her sapphire hair was pulled back from her forehead in thick braids that fell down her back. She wore blue-crystal armor that was molded perfectly to her muscular body and the hilt of a wicked-looking sword stuck up from behind her shoulder.

Was that Kral's mom?

Whoa...

Becca started to worry a little bit about her in-laws. Future in-laws. Whatever.

Them not liking her might be more of a big deal than she'd thought.

Had they traveled all the way out here to talk to Kral? Lar had said something about a transmission. Maybe they could teleport, like in some of the sci-fi shows she watched.

"Kral," the man said. "I thought my instructions were clear."

"They were," Kral said.

"Then what are you still doing in the Sol system?"

"Claiming my soulmate and rescuing her sister," Kral said. "I'm sure Lar has sent you a full report by now."

"Speculation," his father waved a hand dismissively.

Becca felt a spike of irritation from Kral. It added to her own anger, pushing her past the edge of her self-restraint.

"Excuse me, Kevin," Becca said.

"It's Korvin, actually," Kral's dad said.

"Okay," she said. "We have evidence."

Korvin's lip curled up in a very Kral-like snarl. It made it harder for Becca to be afraid of him.

His mom? Yeah. She was still scary as hell. But his dad, not so much.

"Kral," Korvin said. "Who is this?"

Kral put his arm around Becca's shoulders. "This is Becca. My soulmate."

Korvin rolled his eyes, then rubbed his forehead. He let out a weary sigh.

"The Earthling," Korvin said. "Of course, he chose the Earthling."

"Fate chose Becca for me." Kral looked down at her and smiled. "I am therefore the luckiest sentient in the galaxy. I could not have asked for a better partner in this life. Becca has accepted me, and we are bonded."

Korvin stared at them for a few moments, as if trying to process the situation. Kral's mother reached out and placed a hand on Korvin's shoulder.

"It doesn't matter if you're bonded." Her voice was low and had a rich timbre. "Our people will not accept her without the challenge by combat."

"Ehmach," Rom said, "if our soulmates are to be found on Earth, surely we can make allowances—"

"Your soulmates are *not* to be found on Earth," she said. "Earth lacks the technological advancement needed to be a source of mates for our people. They don't even have a single planetary government. What you call making allowances, others would call turning our back on our culture and traditions. There are alternate sources for soulmates."

"Among Sadirians?" Tarn sneered as he said the word.

"Okay, hold on there," Becca said. "My brother is dating a Sadirian, and she's awesome. With Cygnus-Prime facing the population issues you've described, you shouldn't cut yourself off from any possibilities."

Ehmach straightened. "The Earthling speaks well."

"The Earthling has a name," Becca said.

Korvin laughed, then coughed as if he was trying to hide it. He cast a quick glance at Ehmach, who glared at him briefly.

"Kral and Nuar have both found their soulmates here," Dorn said. "We must now find ours on Earth as well."

"Wait, what?" Becca said.

"A prism is connected at a soul level," Ehmach said. "By bonding with Earthlings, Kral and Nuar have doomed their prism to find their soulmates on Earth, or not at all."

"Right. 'Doomed.'" Becca used sarcastic air quotes. "Because Earth is such a shithole. But if it's so bad, how come the Coalition wants to be roommates with us? Why are the Vegans here?"

Ehmach's lips thinned.

"Sorca has bonded with an Earthling," Kral said. "Even after decades of living among Sadirians, she chose an Earthling. And I have bonded with Becca. We must consider the possibility that Earth is where we will find our soulmates, not among the Coalition."

"Or, you know, be open to either?" Becca said. "Why would you limit your people's chances to find happiness?"

"You know nothing of our ways," Ehmach said.

"Then teach us." Becca shrugged. "We're adaptable."

"No amount of teaching will allow you to best Kral in battle." Ehmach stepped forward, her hand clenching into a fist and rising between them.

Okay, so his mom was kinda agro... Really agro. Becca could handle it.

She kept herself from flinching back and instead stepped forward, getting right in the Cygnian woman's face. Or, collarbone. Damn, Kral's mom was tall.

"I already know how to enter battle with Kral," Becca said. "And that's fighting at his side, where I belong."

A wave of love and admiration hit her, strong enough to almost make her sway. She gasped, but quickly recovered, glaring at Ehmach again.

"The only way our people will accept you as their future queen is if you can stand above Kral, holding the Neh'r Golan in your grip, and claiming victory," Ehmach said. "Only then will you have the right to call him mate."

"What the hell is the Neh'r Golan?" Becca asked.

"It's the ceremonial necklace I wear," Kral said. "It marks me as heir to the throne."

"So, let me get this straight," Becca said. "All I have to do to 'marry' Kral in your custom is challenge him, get him on his back, and grab his necklace off of him?"

"'All?'" Korvin said. "Kral is one of our mightiest warriors."

Becca barely kept herself from smirking. She had a lot of ideas for ways to get Kral on his back. She was pretty sure she could distract him well enough to get the necklace off, too.

Becca turned to Kral. "Is that necklace reinforced or anything so that you need super strength to get it off?"

"No," he said.

She turned back to the Ehmach. "Okay, then. I accept your terms, but you have to accept mine."

Ehmach crossed her arms over her chest again and arched an eyebrow.

Korvin shook his head. "You're in no position to demand terms."

"Let her speak," Ehmach said.

Becca mirrored Ehmach's posture. "First, we save my sister. Then, we do the challenge. But I get to choose when and where."

"Becca, you don't have to do this," Kral said.

She angled her head toward him, but kept herself

facing Ehmach. Becca had been in—or avoided—enough fights to know that body language could do a lot to keep a situation from escalating.

Then again, if Ehmach decided to throw down, Becca didn't like her chances. Ehmach looked like she could flatten Becca with both hands tied behind her back. Heck, she looked like she could take on Kral.

"I want to do this," Becca said. "I issue a formal challenge for the right to be Kral's mate. Or whatever. I'm not afraid to accept your terms. Do you accept mine?"

She hoped she wasn't going too far. She'd basically thrown down a gauntlet. If they refused, she was pretty much calling them cowards.

"We accept your terms," Ehmach said, her lips curling away from her very, very sharp teeth. "And we will bear witness to your challenge when you are ready to proceed."

"What now?" Becca said.

Ehmach turned away from Becca, staring at Kral. "Tell us of this evidence you have."

Wait, 'bear witness?'

"We found Tau Ceti blood on Sophie's dog," Kral said.

"Ridiculous." Ehmach shook her head. "There's no way an animal like Pickles could have injured a Tau Ceti badly enough to cause them to bleed. The evidence must have been falsified."

"Pickles is fierce," Kral growled. "And I have no doubt he could pierce the soft flesh of the Tau Ceti."

Damn, Kral had seemed to like Pickles before, but Becca hadn't realized how much. He was up in arms defending the little pom-pom.

"Sophie's dog is a different type of dog," Lar said. He made a sharp whistling sound and Dash came running into the room. She sat at Lar's feet, staring up at him and smiling, as if waiting for the next command.

"Sheesh, you're never that eager to listen to me when I call," Becca said.

Dash barked at her.

"Traitor," Becca murmured.

"This is Sophie's dog," Lar said. "She's known as a Border Collie."

Ehmach arched an eyebrow. "She's larger than Pickles."

"You've met Buddy's dog?" Becca said. So, Buddy wouldn't tell his family he was dating an alien, but he was taking his dog on extra-terrestrial adventures?

Becca was going to give him so much grief for that.

"We haven't met Pickles, but Kral has sent an abundance of imagery," Korvin said. He laughed, and added, "And descriptions that are difficult to believe. Fur as soft and insubstantial as vapor? Please."

"Pomeranians are truly the softest beings in the galaxy." Lar scratched behind Dash's ears. "Not all dogs share that trait. Humans have bred them for a variety of functions, and their appearances are incredibly diverse."

"Genetic engineering?" Korvin leaned forward, obviously intrigued.

"Through selective breeding," Lar said. "They have achieved remarkable results, even with their technological level."

"You must admit that Dash could blood a Tau Ceti," Kral said.

"True," Ehmach said. "But I remain unconvinced that the blood wasn't placed there by someone else. With the fall of the High Council, the Coalition has plunged into chaos. Factions are rising within it, vying for power."

"And these are the people you want to find mates among?" Becca said.

"We could assist them with restoring order," Ehmach snapped.

"So, what, you're going to swoop in and take over?" Becca said. "That sounds like something the High Council would do."

Ehmach's hand lifted toward her sword, her lips peeled back from her teeth in a snarl.

Oh damn.

Korvin grabbed Ehmach's arm. "Now, darling," he said. "We've both already said Earthlings don't understand our ways."

"I understand that everyone has an angle," Becca said. "So what's yours? If you're really just interested in helping your people survive, you should be backing Kral up in trying to figure out who took my sister. Because whoever they are, you can be sure they have an angle, too, and it is not to help the Cygnians out."

Ehmach's eyes were the same orange as Kral's. It was easy to see, with how they were glowing.

Crap, did they have laser powers? Could Kral's mom just disintegrate Becca with a glare?

She'd be sure to ask as soon as these guys left. If Becca survived that long.

"We will send three ships," Ehmach said. "Someone is trying to play us for fools, whether it be the Coalition or the Assembly. Once we know for certain, we will make them pay."

Becca stepped forward and rose on her tip-toes, trying to get as close to "in her face" with Ehmach as she could. Her heart was pounding. Becca hoped the Cygnians couldn't hear it, since that would definitely impact her attempt at bravado.

In a low voice, she said, "Not if we find them first."

Ehmach lowered her head, her teeth bared in what might have been a smile? That was progress, right?

"You have twelve Earth hours until we strike and depart," Ehmach said. "The Cygnian people have other concerns."

In the blink of an eye, Ehmach, Korvin, and even their furniture disappeared.

"Whoa, what the hell?" Becca said, staggering back a

few paces and flailing her arms. Kral caught her before she could completely lose her balance and fall on her ass. "Where did they go?"

Lar looked around the room. "They were never here. It was a holoprojection."

"You're kidding." Becca shook her head. "I would have sworn they were in the room."

Kral arched an eyebrow. "You thought my mother, Queen Ehmach, was in the room when you were challenging her like that?"

"Well... yeah," Becca said.

"Few would be brave enough to do so," Lar said.

"Or foolish," Dorn added.

Becca cast a withering glare his way. "She was pissing me off."

"Issuing challenge to me was completely unnecessary." Kral spun her around to face him. "We have claimed each other, and that's enough."

"Maybe if you were just any Cygnian, it would be," she said. "But you're not. You're the prince. Your people need to accept me if I'm going to..."

Holy shit.

If she was going to what? Be their queen some day?

She was still riding high off the post-sex endorphins. What had she gotten herself into?

It was probably more of a ceremonial thing. The king held the power and the queen was like...an advisor or something. Kral couldn't possibly think that Becca would eventually be one of his people's leaders. She just wanted to be with him.

Still, her mind was spinning with possibilities, trying to come up with a plan to get that necklace off Kral's neck.

"What was that part about witnesses?" she asked.

"It is custom that for a royal union, the battle is broadcast to a large segment of our population," Lar said.

Oh shit. There went her plan to use her sexy wiles to get Kral on his back. No way was she doing that in front of his whole planet.

She stepped away from him, trying to clear her thoughts.

The challenge was a problem for another time. For now, they needed to find Sophie. They only had twelve hours to do so.

"Look, this all falls firmly into the 'tomorrow's problem' category," she said. "Right now, we need to focus on finding Sophie."

"I agree," Lar said.

Kral leaned in close. "This conversation isn't over."

"Of course it isn't," she said. "But it's not something we can fix right now, so let's focus on what's right in front of us."

Lar struck his wristbands together. Dozens of asteroids appeared in the center of the room. Big ones, little ones, medium-sized ones. They floated peacefully through space, as if none of them could possibly hide a base where bad guy aliens were up to nefarious plans.

Becca reached out to touch one. Her fingers passed through the rocky surface. Again, she would have sworn it was right there in the room with them.

She stepped closer to the wall so she could see more of the display. The room was completely filled with rocks, floor to ceiling.

"There are so many," she murmured.

Kral put an arm around her shoulder. "Don't worry. We'll find her."

Becca nodded, her eyes scanning the images in front of her, as if that would be enough. Somewhere in all of that, Sophie was waiting to be rescued.

"We better get to it," Becca said.

Chapter Eighteen

"Twelve hours isn't much time," Lar said. "Your mother will not be as...restrained as we would be."

"What does that mean?" Becca's voice was laced with anxiety.

"It means we need to hurry," Kral said.

"Have we scanned sector G-26 yet?" Lar asked.

Kral came to stand beside Lar, looking at the section of the asteroid field his friend was focused on. The other members of the prism had returned to their stations, checking the ship's systems and preparing for whatever might lie ahead. Kral had also secured a new set of wristbands for himself.

Bron spoke over the ship's communication channel. "Some time ago."

"Why isn't Bron in here?" Becca was on Kral's other side. "Does he need some kind of science gizmos to do his work?"

"He could work from anywhere in the ship," Kral said. "But Bron prefers a quiet workspace with fewer distractions."

Becca looked around the room. She arched an eyebrow,

then shrugged. "It did seem a bit crowded in here earlier. I still can't believe I thought your parents were in the room with us."

"I still can't believe you challenged my mother when you thought you were within her range of attack." Kral laughed, knowing his mother wouldn't actually hurt Becca.

She might have tussled, though.

Becca gave a little shiver. "Is she always that agro?"

"Agro?" Kral asked.

"Aggressive," Becca said.

"She's the warrior-queen of the Cygnian race," Lar said. "How else would she be?" He was still staring at that one section of the field.

"What is it, brother?" Kral asked.

Lar shook his head. "I'm not sure. There's something about this asteroid that seems off to me. A feeling more than an observation."

Kral hummed the note that opened the channel to the cockpit. "Rom, take us closer to sector G-26. I want a surface scan of this asteroid."

"Understood," Rom said.

Kral tapped the asteroid that had caught Lar's attention. The holodisplay stopped showing any others and zoomed in on just the one, showing their ship's approach.

Lar glanced over at Kral and Kral shrugged.

"Your instincts have always served us well," Kral said.

"I see no reason to start doubting them now."

They watched the hologram as they drew closer to their target, the *Arrow* flying close to the surface. The asteroid was easily large enough to house a facility within its depths—deeper than the Coalition could detect.

As they scanned the asteroid, the display stripped away its outer layers. Rom flew the ship around and around the rock, circling it at slightly different angles to make sure their scans were complete.

"What's that?" Lar stepped forward and activated his wristband's interface with the display, then grabbed the hologram of the asteroid, stopping its movement. He spun the image around. Beneath an outcropping of rock as big as a small mountain on Earth, a large opening led beneath the asteroid's surface.

"None of the readings indicate synthetic materials in the tunnel," Kral said.

"It could be natural." Lar stared intently at the spot. "But the dimensions would accommodate many types of Tau Ceti ships, even the less streamlined ones."

Kral turned to Becca and said, "The Tau Ceti often have triangular designs to their ships, as well as long sort of stems beneath the main decks. It's somewhat like dandelion seeds."

"Sounds kind of pretty," Becca said.

"Then I'm describing it wrong," Kral said.

"Tau Ceti cruisers are difficult to navigate in

atmospheres," Lar said. "And they require very particular sizes and shapes for openings for their larger ships to enter and leave."

"You're right that this would work." Kral activated the link to Rom again. "Rom, take us into that cave system. Make sure our shielding and cloaks are at maximum power."

"We're locked down tight, but I'll keep an eye on it," Rom said.

Lar released the holodisplay and stepped back. The image showed their ship descending into the asteroid, then switched to an interior view.

After several bends and swerves that would absolutely stump Coalition sensors, they saw what they were looking for.

"Is that..." Becca stepped closer to the display.

"It is," Kral said.

The tunnel opened up into an enormous cavern—one that could easily hold several base ships. But they didn't need a base ship. They were using the asteroid instead.

Dozens of Tau Ceti vessels rested on the cavern's floor, walls, and ceiling. The *Arrow* drifted in among them.

Kral activated the ship-wide communication channel and left it open. "Bron."

"I'm modifying the scans as we speak," Bron said.

The display flickered, an overlay of data scrolling next to the images they saw, along with outlines appearing around possible points of interest.

"There." Lar pointed to a section of wall that was too smooth to be natural. The scan highlighted it a moment after Lar pointed it out. "That must be their main entry point."

"If that's their main entrance, it'll be monitored," Becca said. "We should try to find a back door, so we don't spook them into doing something rash."

"It doesn't matter where we enter their base from," Kral said. "Once they see us, they'll sound the alarm."

"Don't you have, like, personal cloaks?" she asked. "I mean, you already have those holograms."

"That are only meant to disguise our appearance, not turn us invisible," Kral said.

"Can you modify them to act as cloaks?" she asked.

"Unfortunately not," Lar said.

"We are warriors," Kral said. "We stride into battle, we don't hide from it."

"I'm not saying you should hide, I'm saying you should be strategic." Becca studied the display intently. "This is another door, right?"

She pointed at a smooth section of wall that was indeed another opening.

"Yes," Kral said.

"Can we see inside the base?" Becca asked.

"Bringing it up now," Bron said.

The display of the inside of the cavern winked out.

Another map appeared, this one made of rooms and corridors that were outlined in light. As the scans progressed, more data was added.

"I wish I could read your language," Becca said, watching the data flickering around the display.

Before Kral could reach out to Bron, the readouts changed to Becca's language.

"Oh, wow," she said. "Thanks."

Colored dots appeared, moving about the map.

"Are those people?" Becca asked.

"Yes," Kral said. "The yellowish-green signifies a regular Tau Ceti soldier. Dark green are ones that are cybernetically enhanced."

"Cyborgs?" she said. "Should I be worried for you guys?"

Kral snorted. "Of course not."

She stood a little straighter. "Should I be concerned you're not going to let me go along?"

What a strange question. But as Kral thought of her culture, it made more sense.

"You've met my mother," Kral said. "She is the leader of all our armies. The fiercest warrior among us. I would never deny you the chance to go into battle at my side, especially when we're trying to rescue your sister."

"Oh." Becca's cheeks turned a little pink. "Good."

"Sophie…" Lar nearly gasped the word.

Becca spun around as Kral also sought the one glowing

golden dot among all the others.

She was being held in a line of small chambers deep in the base. They would have to pass several checkpoints to get there.

A bit deeper on, the chambers became larger, but with reinforced walls and heavier shielding. Kral's hearts chilled as he considered their use.

Laboratories.

A rattling noise brought his attention back to Lar. His spine plates had risen and were vibrating against each other. He must have come to the same conclusion.

"Lar, it'll be okay," Becca said. "We're going to rescue her."

She had no idea what had set Lar off. Kral couldn't bring himself to explain. Not yet.

Sophie hadn't been with them for long. Hopefully, she hadn't seen the inside of one of those chambers. Kral intended to make sure she never did.

"We go now," Lar said. "*Now.*"

Kral nodded, but turned to Becca. "You'll need weapons and armor. Our artisans will grow you a set of crystal armor as soon as they can. In the meantime, we'll see what we have here."

"We're not going to just charge in there," Becca said. "They might panic and kill Sophie."

"We can't just sit here," Kral said. "The longer we wait, the worse it will be for her."

"What do you mean?" she asked.

"Just trust me when I say we have to go now," Kral said.

"Fine." Becca's eyes narrowed. "But we're still not crashing through the door."

"What do you have in mind?" Kral asked.

"Your wristbands can make you look like Earthlings," she said.

"Yes." He tried to keep the impatience from his voice.

"Can they make you look like a Tau Ceti?" she asked.

Kral did not like where this was going.

Becca kept on, apparently taking his silence as confirmation. "If you can use your holo-wristband things to look like a Tau Ceti, you could escort me into the place as if I'm your prisoner."

Who would think of such a plan? Especially when they were the one most at risk.

"That won't work," Kral said. "They'd want to process you and we would undoubtedly be separated."

"Not if they think I've already been processed," she said. "Think about it. We're pretty sure they were after me, right?"

"All the more reason to not hand you over to them," Kral said.

"I'm not saying that we do." A devious smile lit her features. "They took Sophie because they couldn't tell us apart. What if you walk me to that line of cells where they're keeping her, pretending that you're returning Sophie to where she's supposed to be?"

Kral did not like this plan. He had many reasons for not liking this plan. His spine plates started to rise just thinking of the danger she'd be placing herself in.

"They want me," Becca said. "They're keeping Sophie alive. I don't think they'll hurt us unless someone panics."

After a few moments, Dorn's voice sounded over the comm. "It's a good plan."

Becca beamed, but Kral shook his head, scowling.

"Many things could go wrong," Kral said.

"How is that different than any other battle?" Becca asked. "Even as tough and strong as you are, there is always a chance that things won't go the way you want. There's always an element of risk."

"But I've never had a soulmate at stake before," he said.

Becca crossed her arms. "Oh, so I'm only allowed to walk into battle at your side if you're sure we'll win?"

Kral growled. Becca didn't back down.

"I want you to fight at my side," Kral said. "But I also want to keep you safe."

"As long as they have my sister, I'm not safe," she said. "Think of how you'd feel if it was one of your prism in there."

Honestly, he would feel quite a bit better. His men were accomplished warriors, and the Tau Ceti lacked the technology to do them harm.

Kral had to remember, though, that the Assembly might. The Centaurans had secret weapons and heightened capabilities that they might have already shared with the Tau Ceti in this base.

"What if it was your sister?" Becca asked.

The thought nearly pushed him over the edge, especially when he considered those laboratories. Sorca had spent too much of her life at the mercy of Coalition scientists, and the Tau Ceti were so much worse.

"You're not a Cygnian," Kral said.

"So, let's make that work in our favor," Becca said.

"We don't have time to argue," Lar said. "It is her right to accompany us into battle, and each warrior chooses how they equip themselves. Her plan is sound."

Kral *hated* this plan. But he didn't see another way.

He turned to Becca and said, "The Tau Ceti look just like Sadirians and Earthlings. With our holo-emitters and Earth clothing, we can pass for one of them easily."

"But we'll need to pass for three," Lar said. "The Tau Ceti always work in triads."

"You, me, and Bron," Kral said.

Lar shook his head. "Dorn won't like that."

"I need him here guarding the ship," Kral said. He knew the intership channel was still open, so he added, "Dorn, your priority is keeping Amy and Dash safe."

"Understood," Dorn said.

That was easier than Kral had expected. Relieved, he went on.

"Rom, land us close to that back door," Kral said.

"Already did," Rom said. "Landed so smooth, you didn't even notice it."

"I've also accessed their security feeds," Bron said. "We'll have five minutes to get inside and deep enough into the complex to avoid suspicion when we show up on their vids."

Kral grinned. His prism was the greatest fighting force the Cygnians had. They would find Sophie and bring her home and keep Becca safe doing so.

"Then let's go," Becca said.

"Here's your route," Dorn said.

A blue light appeared on the map showing the hallway beyond the door they'd be using. It turned and twisted as it passed along the corridors leading to Sophie's cell. After arriving, there was a flash, and a darker blue light turned and traced a different route back out.

"The way in is longer, but has fewer check-points," Dorn said. "The way out takes you along the thinnest walls."

Kral grinned. "We'll blast our way through if necessary."

"My scans show these walls are Tau Ceti in origin," Bron said. "No modifications. We can cut through them with our *swords* if we need to."

"No swords," Kral said. "Remember, we're trying to pass for Tau Ceti."

"Be sure not to use big words, then," Rom said. "These guys don't exactly breed for intelligence."

Kral laughed. He turned to Lar and Becca and said, "Warriors, commit the route to memory."

Her eyes widened and she stood straighter. Then she turned to the display and started studying it intently.

"Our wristbands will show us the route as well," Kral said.

He clanged them together, and hummed a few notes that modified his display. The wristbands and his necklace vanished, concealed by the same hologram that changed his coloration. He altered the settings a bit to make his appearance match that of a Tau Ceti cybernetic soldier a bit more, adding a greenish tint to his skin and fading the dark brown of his hair.

As much as he hated to do so, he also made the hologram conceal his beard. He'd never seen a Tau Ceti with more than just a bit of stubble. At least without his beard, he could also make his mouth appear wider and thin out his lips.

He looked over at Lar and saw that he'd done much the same.

Becca grimaced when she looked at them. "That is just wrong."

"It's temporary," Kral said.

"I should freaking hope so." She shuddered. "What about the eyes?"

"There's nothing we can do about that," Kral said. "Hopefully, they won't notice."

Becca opened her mouth as if to speak, but then snapped it shut. She shook her head, then said, "We'll deal with it if it comes up."

Dorn entered the common room, carrying another set of wristbands. He tossed them to Lar, then walked over to Becca. Gripping her arms, he lifted them, then struck her wristbands together.

"That's how you activate them," Dorn said. "You control them by humming certain notes."

He made a pitch, high enough for Becca to hear, then said, "Shields."

When he nodded, she emulated the sound. Gold light snapped over her body, a few millimeters above her skin.

"Oh yeah," she said. "These are handy." She cast a heat-filled gaze at Kral and smirked.

"The shield also has an atmospheric generator that will kick in when necessary." Dorn hummed another note. A moment later, an overlay of Tau Ceti manacles concealed them.

"Oh, cool." Becca held her hands apart, then moved her wrists closer, watching as the hologram made it look like they were chained together when they actually weren't. "Thanks."

"Kral and Lar can control them as well," Dorn said. "Make sure Sophie puts on the extra pair before she tries to walk across the cavern to the ship. She'll need them to breathe and withstand the cold and radiation."

"What about weapons?" Becca asked.

Kral's hearts warmed. She was truly his match.

Dorn hummed a note that deactivated her wristbands. "Strike them together once, then use this note."

He struck his own wristbands together, then made the sound to activate their weapons—again, using a higher version that she could hear. His wristbands flashed with a soft white light.

He aimed his arm at the wall with his fingers splayed, then squeezed his hand into a fist with a pulling motion. A blast of much brighter light flew from the top of his wristband and hit the wall. The energy spread over the crystal surface and dissipated.

"Oh, wow," Becca said.

Dorn nodded at the spot he'd hit. "Show me."

"What, like now?" she asked.

"I'm not sending you into battle with a weapon you've never used before," Dorn said. "This will even affect a Cygnian, though not as strongly as other sentients."

"I guess that makes sense." Becca shifted into a fighting stance, staring at the wall.

She cleared her throat, then struck her wristbands together. She hummed the note Dorn had given her.

Splaying her fingers, she repeated his movement fairly well. A smaller blast spiraled out from her wristband and hit the floor.

"Shit," Becca said. "What did I do wrong?"

"The intensity of your gesture controls the intensity of the blast," Dorn said. "You have the basics. Just make sure that if you use it that you *mean* it, and you'll be fine."

"Gee, thanks," she said.

Kral would have sworn he saw the corner of Dorn's mouth twitch up. Before he could be sure, Dorn turned and exited the room.

Bron entered the common room from another corridor just as Becca said, "Well, he's delightful."

"You get used to him." Bron didn't even slow as he crossed the chamber, heading for the main hatch below.

Lar followed him. Becca started after them as well, but Kral caught her elbow and pulled her close.

"Are you sure you want to do this?" he asked.

"I'm sure I don't want to," she said. "But they have my sister, so I'm going to do it anyway. Besides, you're going. So I go, too."

He smiled at her and said, "So fierce," then leaned in for a quick kiss.

She pushed at his chest after only a moment.

"Save it for when we get back," she said. "We need to focus."

"Of course."

He followed her through the ship, amazed at how well she fit into his world. She was commanding, bold, and aggressive. A perfect mate for him.

Blast doors closed on either side of them as they stood before a small hatch. They each struck their wristbands together and activated their shielding, even Becca.

"Nicely done," Lar said.

Becca grinned at him. "Good thing I can carry a tune."

They all laughed.

This was yet another way she was fitting into his life. His prism had already fully accepted her.

Kral's hearts beat with new strength. Becca was part of him now and so was her family. They would rescue Sophie, then let his mother have her fun turning this place to dust.

The airlock finished decompressing just before the hatch opened. Kral took Becca's elbow and held her as the gravity lessened. He pulled her against his side and watched as the other two men pushed off from the ship, speeding across the short distance between the *Arrow* and the back door to the facility.

He could feel her heart beating quickly. Her skin had paled a bit. Those were the only signs of her fear.

Better to get this done quickly.

He maneuvered them to the outer hull of the ship, then pushed off from it, following the other warriors. Bron timed opening the door to the Tau Ceti base perfectly, so that Kral and Becca floated straight through. He and Lar entered behind them.

As soon as the door closed, decon lights hit their bodies. An artificial gravity field took effect as the hiss of air entering the chamber surrounded them.

Kral knew Bron would have masked this from the Tau Ceti sentries as well while covering up their arrival. Still, the moment the airlock had finished its cycling, he was through the door and heading down a corridor.

"Kral," Bron said.

Kral looked over his shoulder. Bron nodded toward Becca, still tucked against Kral's side.

"Right." Kral gave her a squeeze, then released her and quickened his stride.

"Stay between us," Lar said. "Kral will lead and Bron and I will only be a few paces behind you."

"Have Bron be in front," she said.

The warriors paused and gazed at her.

"Blue eyes." She pointed at her own. "If the Tau Ceti can pass for human, blue eyes isn't as much of a stretch, even if they're kinda...glowy. Orange and yellow, not so much. You guys are in the back. Keep your heads down."

She held her arms together, making the hologram covering her wristbands look like she was in manacles, then turned and started walking down the corridor. Kral nodded to Bron, who hurried to be in front of her.

Kral felt his chest swell with pride. Her strategic

strength would be a gift to the Cygnians.

He turned his focus ahead as they followed the route that Dorn had laid out for them. The first two sentry posts they passed didn't even look up from their stations.

The third...

Kral felt his spine plates stir as he recognized the faces of the Tau Ceti sitting behind the desk. And these three definitely were paying attention.

"What the hell do you think you're doing?" The tallest one stood and walked around his station, getting right in Bron's face—just as he'd gotten in Becca's face back on Earth.

These were three of the men from the sub shop who had been harassing her. Kral held his breath, hoping they wouldn't recognize him or Lar.

There had been four of them in the shop. But Tau Ceti were always assigned in triads. Where—or what—was the fourth?

"Who authorized you to take the Earthling out of her cell?" the Tau Ceti said.

"Guys, we can not screw up again," one of the other Tau Ceti said. "They'll throw us into the feeding tanks."

"Shut up, Tobek," the first Tau Ceti said. "This isn't our screw up. It's theirs."

Bron managed to look confused. "We...um... We're just supposed to take her back to her cell." He shrugged. "I don't know where she was before she was handed over to us. Maybe they were uh…using her in the labs?"

He heard Becca's quick intake of breath. Kral probably should have told her about the labs before they'd left. It was too late now.

"The labs are that way." The leader of the triad pointed behind him, the way Kral and his group had been heading.

Bron looked over his shoulder, then looked back. He smiled, and said, "We got a little turned around. It's this way?"

"Tobek," the guy snapped. "Show these idiots where the holding cells are and make sure the Earthling is secured."

"Sure." Tobek jumped up and started down the corridor at a brisk pace.

Kral and his warriors could easily keep up, but Becca had to almost run to match their strides.

"What's the hurry?" Kral asked, trying to keep his voice as vacuous as possible.

"My triad screwed up big time with this Earthling," Tobek said. "Rixon is probably reporting you right now to make sure we don't end up as fodder for the next generation of Tau Ceti."

"That's just…an expression, right?" Becca asked. "They wouldn't really eat you."

Tobek looked over his shoulder at her and shrugged. "I've been telling you, our ways are very different."

He'd been talking to Sophie?

If he'd spent time with her, he was more likely to be able to realize that Becca wasn't the Earthling he thought she was. Bron must have had the same thought. He stepped to the side, trying to block Tobek's view of her.

"If we can get her back in her cell before Rixon reports you, then maybe none of us will get in trouble," Tobek said.

"That's…decent of you," Lar said.

"Yeah, well, you can make fun of me for it if we all live through this," Tobek said.

He led them through a room filled with cages of various sizes. Their walls were little more than thickened wires.

Kral had never seen such a low-tech prison. What kind of beings were they keeping and for what purpose?

They finally stopped in front of a solid metal door with a window grate a bit below his eye level. There was another grate lower down that was probably used to pass items into the room.

There was an access panel next to the door. Tobek entered a code—without bothering to try to hide the sequence from their view—then pressed his palm against the scanner.

The door clicked and swung out into the hallway.

"Here you are, So…phie?" His eyes widened as he saw the Earthling sitting on a bench along the wall inside the room, then turned back to Becca.

Kral didn't give him a chance to make another sound. He grabbed Tobek by his throat and lifted him off his feet as he entered the cell, followed quickly by Lar and Becca. Bron waited in the hall to ensure they didn't all get locked inside.

"Thank you for your assistance," Kral said, tightening his grip.

Chapter Nineteen

The moment Becca crossed into the room, she ran to Sophie's side and threw her arms around her sister. Tried to, anyway.

Sophie stiffened, pushing away from the hug.

"Sophie," Becca said. "Sophie, are you okay?"

"Put him down," Sophie yelled. "Put him down, please!"

Kral looked over at them, confusion obvious on his features, then slowly set Tobek on his feet. Kral kept a hold on the Tau Ceti's neck, though.

"We need to go," Lar said. He struck his wristbands together, then ran his hands through the air in front of Sophie, scanning her. "You seem in good health."

"I'm fine." She eyed Lar warily. "But I'm not going anywhere with you."

What the hell was going on?

"They're with me," Becca said. "These are my friends. This is Kral." She turned to him, and said, "Can you change your hologram to what you looked like at our family dinner?"

"Of course." Kral let go of Tobek, who staggered back

a few paces.

Kral struck his wristbands together. The hologram changed back to his appearance when they'd first met.

"Surfer dude," Sophie gasped.

"It's *Kral*," Becca corrected. "And I *so* have dibs on him."

Sophie scowled at her. Now, that was a bit more normal. Becca had been close to freaking out with how stand-offish Sophie was being before.

"We are bonded." Kral turned to Tobek and said, "And if anyone should try to harm her or any members of her family again, they will face the full wrath of the Cygnians."

Tobek swallowed with seeming difficulty. He looked back and forth between Sophie and Kral.

"That sounds fair," Tobek said.

Sophie pushed away from Becca and moved to stand between them. "Leave him alone."

"You would protect your captor?" Kral said.

Becca followed after Sophie, trying to grab her arm. Sophie shook her off.

"Honey, I think you have Stockholm syndrome," Becca said. Although, it seemed like there hadn't been enough time for that to develop.

"I do not have Stockholm syndrome," Sophie spat. "You sound like..." Her eyes widened. "Amy. Is Amy okay?"

"She's fine," Becca said. "We reached her in time."

"Where is she?" Sophie asked.

"She's on Kral's ship," Becca said.

"And Dash?" Sophie's voice shook a little with the question. "Is she okay? Did you make sure she got in her run? She gets anxious if she doesn't keep to her agility practice schedule."

Becca rolled her eyes. "Oh my god, you're obsessed with that dog. She's fine. Now can we please get you out of here?"

Sophie looked at Tobek with a pained expression. He shook his head briefly.

"What the hell is going on here?" Becca demanded. "You should be running out of this place screaming, not digging in your heels."

"It's complicated," Sophie said. "There's more going on than you realize."

"Then sum it up," Becca nearly yelled.

Bron stuck his head through the doorway. "If we want any chance of walking out of here instead of blasting our way out, we need to go."

Lar approached Sophie with the set of wristbands Dorn had given him. She lurched back.

"It's okay," Becca said. "These will keep you safe when we're out of the base. We have to cross through some…space I guess, to get to their ship."

"Prove that you're a Cygnian," Sophie said, tilting up

her chin.

Lar glanced over at Kral, who shrugged.

"Sophie, we don't have time for this," Becca said. "Please."

Sophie picked up a metal tray from the bench where she'd been sitting. She dumped the dishes off of it, then swung it as hard as she could at Lar.

He didn't try to block it. Didn't even flinch away.

The tray bent over his head. The impact didn't move him so much as an inch.

He lifted his arms and struck his wristbands together. The hologram covering him vanished—leaving him his actual cobalt-blue.

Sophie's eyes widened and her mouth dropped open. Becca recognized that far-off look, and they absolutely did not have time for it.

"What the hell, Sophie?" Becca said. "Let Lar put those wristbands on you, or I swear I will have him throw you over his shoulder and carry you out of here."

That might not have been the best tack to take. Sophie actually leaned a bit forward, as if she liked the idea.

Lar slid the wristbands onto her wrists, smiling as they shrank to fit her.

"Great." Becca turned to the door. "Let's go."

"Wait," Sophie yelled.

"For the love of…" Becca yelled. "What is it now?"

"They'll kill Tobek if he lets me get away," Sophie

said.

"'Lets you?'" Kral said. "He doesn't have a choice in the matter."

"His bosses won't see it that way," Sophie said.

"Do you want us to take him, too?" Lar asked.

"Lar," Kral yelled.

Becca hadn't seen the prism fight yet, but she had a feeling if there was time, these two would be throwing down. Luckily, Sophie jumped in.

"No," Sophie said. "He needs to be here."

"What did they do to you?" Becca asked.

Sophie opened her mouth, then snapped it shut. Her eyes filled with tears.

Fury filled Becca's heart.

Something had happened. Something beyond being kidnapped by aliens and watching their sister get shot. And Becca didn't have enough time to figure out what was wrong and fix it. They had to go.

"We have to leave," Lar said. "We can't afford to get pinned in here. Three Cygnian warships are merely hours away, intent on destroying this base."

"Lar!" This time, Kral grabbed Lar by the shoulder and threw him. Lar hit the wall of the small room, denting the metal.

"I won't tell anyone," Tobek said, stepping forward.

Lar and Kral both turned to him. Tobek just shrugged.

"It'll be a lot quicker and less...messy if the Cygnians

kill me," Tobek said. "Either way, it's gonna happen."

Becca was starting to feel for the guy. Maybe it wasn't too soon for Sophie to have Stockholm syndrome.

"Shut up, Tobek." Sophie grabbed his arms and shook him. "You can't give up. I need you alive and I need you here. You tell them that you befriended me. That you were able to get me to like you so much that I told you about the attack. Tell them that they can use our friendship to get to me. To get to Becca and the Cygnians. You tell them whatever you need to for them to keep trusting you. To stay alive."

"I'll do what I can," he said. "But you'd better get out of here."

"Is there anything we can do to assist with your story?" Becca asked.

Whatever was going on with her sister, Sophie was right. It was complicated and there was more going on than Becca knew. But if she wanted a chance to find out, she would have to trust Sophie and back her up.

"It'd be a lot more believable if the others actually saw three Cygnian warriors busting their way out of here," Tobek said.

Kral smiled, then struck his wristbands together, dropping his hologram. "That is a plan I can get behind."

"Then let's get out of here," Becca said. She grabbed Sophie's arm and pulled her to the door.

Once they were out in the hall, Kral shut the door,

sealing Tobek in. Becca gave him a questioning look.

"They would kill him immediately if they thought he'd just let us leave," Kral said.

That made sense, she guessed.

"Do we need to...rough him up or something?" Becca hated suggesting it, but felt she had too.

Through the door, she heard Tobek say, "I'm a cyborg. We heal quickly so that wouldn't really help."

"Then let's go," Lar said.

Bron had already dropped his hologram as well. His left arm was covered in a rippling blue energy field that extended out in a flat disc three feet across.

"Is that another kind of shield?" Becca asked. "Can ours do that?"

Lar struck his wristbands together and hummed a note. The same energy field popped out of his wristband, only on his right arm.

"Sophie." Becca followed Lar's example, and a shield appeared on her left arm. Sophie nodded and did the same. Thank God their mother had insisted they all learn to sing.

Becca was glad Sophie was finally listening to her. Maybe they had a chance of getting out of this after all.

Kral led them back down the corridor, but took a different turn. Becca was right behind him, with Sophie following. Lar and Bron brought up the rear.

When Becca glanced back, she saw that both men were keeping their shields up and covering them. Which meant that Becca and Kral were covering the front.

Actually, she was the one covering the front, since Kral hadn't activated his shield. It was amazing to have a partner who actually treated her like a fully functional adult and wasn't threatened by her.

She heard yelling ahead, then the scuffling of booted feet approaching from around the corner. Time to earn the trust and faith he was putting in her. She lifted her arm, keeping herself in front of Sophie and the others as much as she could.

Kral stopped twenty feet from the turn. He struck his wristbands together. Instead of lowering his arms, as usual, he kept them together, rubbing the wristbands in circles. As he did, he hummed a low note that reverberated through her chest. It reminded her of a Tibetan Singing Bowl.

As he held the note, the vibration built, until the floor was shaking beneath them. The air in front of him rippled like a heat mirage.

Half a dozen Tau Ceti soldiers ran around the corner. The moment they were all in the corridor, Kral pushed both his hands forward in a sharp motion. A shockwave blasted out from him that dented the walls, ceiling, and floor of the corridor.

The Tau Ceti were blown off their feet, flying toward the wall at the end of the corridor. The ones in back hit with a sickening crunch. Green blood pooled around them.

Kral strode forward. Becca and Sophie had to run to keep up with his long gait. He finally activated his shield just as the next batch of Tau Ceti appeared at the end of the next corridor.

The cyborgs saw their group, along with the pile of bodies behind the Cygnian warriors, and froze. The triad in front backed up a pace. They glanced at each other, then turned and ran.

"That's a good thing, right?" Sophie asked.

A thick door descended from the ceiling and crashed to the ground in front of them, blocking the entire corridor.

"You had to say something," Becca said.

"No worries." Lar smiled at them, then turned to Bron.

The warriors nodded to each other and deactivated their shields. Becca moved so that she was guarding Sophie's other side as Kral shielded them from the front.

Lar and Bron struck their wristbands together. The air around them started to ripple. They pointed their hands at the wall, like Dorn had taught Becca earlier, then curled their hands into fists and made the pulling motion.

Blinding light shot out from their wristbands, hitting the metal wall and making it glow. Becca had to shield her eyes, it was so bright. When she could finally look again, a large section of the wall was just gone.

"Whoa," Sophie said.

"The Cygnians are feared with very good reason," Lar said. He bowed and gestured to the hole, the metal around the edges glowing red.

Bron shook his head and stepped through first. Sophie and Becca followed, with Lar and Kral bringing up the rear this time.

They made their way through the maze of corridors more quickly. Bron hacked the security panels or Lar just blasted through the doors between them and the back entrance they'd used when they arrived. Finally, they were at the airlock.

She welcomed the golden light rushing over her skin that let her know the atmospheric generator and shielding were working. Relief flooded her when Sophie activated her own. Becca felt even better when the door opened and she could see the *Arrow* in front of them.

She wanted to hold Sophie's hand as they crossed the space between the door and the ship, but didn't think that would be safe. Kral tucked Becca against his side and Lar held tight to Sophie.

They launched themselves from the door, landing inside the Cygnian vessel. The moment the hatch sealed behind them, she felt a lurching in her stomach. The ship rocked violently, almost throwing her from her feet. The corridor on the other side of the doors sealing them into the space in front of the hatch glowed with blue light.

"Rom," Kral said.

Rom's voice replied over the ship's intercom. "It's going to be a bit bumpy. Hold on tight."

Kral kept his grip around Becca's waist, turning so his back was pressed against Lar's. Lar was still holding onto Sophie. The warriors braced themselves against the corridor with their legs and their one free arm against the wall, carefully holding Becca and her sister in place. Bron braced himself with his arms and legs against the ceiling and floor.

The ship lurched again. Becca would have hit the wall if Kral hadn't been holding her in place.

"Are they shooting at us?" Becca asked.

"Of course they are." Kral grinned.

"Then why are you smiling?" Becca said.

"Because Sophie is safe and we'll be on our way back to Earth in moments," he said. "Not even the Assembly will risk the wrath of the Vegans, and the moment we're clear of the asteroid, we'll be in full view of their sensors."

With one final lurch, the blue light around them faded to the normal soft white. The walls that had created the temporary airlock slid back into the ceiling.

Rom's voice sounded again. "Fun time's over, guys. Let's get these ladies back to Earth."

Kral released his grip on Becca and stood along with Lar and Sophie.

"I'm so glad you're okay." Becca threw her arms around Sophie, hugging her tight. Sophie gripped the back of Becca's shirt and buried her face in Becca's shoulder.

After a few moments, Sophie stepped back. She wiped

at her eyes and sniffed.

Becca heard a sharp bark. Dash came running down the corridor. She kept barking, leaping up at Sophie. For once, Sophie didn't bother trying to make her calm down.

"Dash!" Sophie dropped to her knees next to her dog and grabbed her in a huge hug.

Dash licked her face until Sophie abruptly stiffened. She stood, then gave the hand signal for Dash to sit. The dog immediately complied, tilting her head at Sophie as if she was as confused as Becca by Sophie's weird behavior.

"Can I see Amy?" Sophie asked in a low voice.

"Sure," Becca said. "I can take you."

"It's okay," Sophie said. "I'm sure you have stuff to do. Can…" She looked around, her gaze settling on Lar. "Can you take me?"

"Of course," Lar said.

Becca couldn't believe it. "Sophie, what the hell? This isn't you."

Sophie let out a sharp laugh and her eyes filled with tears again. "Who is themselves anymore?" She pulled herself together with obvious effort. "I just… I'm dealing with some stuff right now. I need time to sort things out."

"I… Okay," Becca said. "But I'm here for you."

"Yeah." Sophie smiled at her, but it was so forced. "I'll see you in a bit."

Sophie and Lar walked away, leaving Becca and Kral alone in the corridor. Kral reached out and rested his hand on her shoulder. Becca turned and pressed her face against his chest.

She'd never been the one who sought support. She was always the one giving it. But turning to Kral felt as natural as breathing. He wrapped his arms around her as she clung to his waist.

"Give her the time she's asked for," Kral said. "She'll come to you when she's ready."

Becca nodded and stepped away. She kept one arm around his waist as he kept her tucked against his side. They walked like that to the common room.

Once they arrived, Kral sat on a bench and pulled her down next to him. She leaned against his chest, exhaustion finally catching up with her.

How long had it been since she'd slept? It was hard to keep her eyes open.

Bron entered the room and spoke in a hushed voice. "I've sent all the data we gathered to your parents."

"Did you tell them the Tau Ceti know they're coming?" Kral said, also keeping his voice low. Becca liked the way it rumbled through his chest into her ear. That and the strong beat of his hearts was soothing.

"I told them we needed to warn a guard to rescue Sophie safely," Bron said.

"How did they take it?" Kral asked.

Bron just shrugged.

Kral chuckled. "I'm beginning to understand why the

Earthlings keep secrets."

"It isn't as though the king and queen weren't keeping secrets from us," Bron said. "From all of us. I respectfully reminded her that they can't just vaporize the asteroid, as well. As primitive as Earth technology is, they would likely notice if an asteroid of that size went missing. They actually call this one a dwarf planet and have a name for it. Ceres."

Kral shifted a bit, leaning against the wall. Their conversation became more and more fuzzy, just a rumbling of deep voices washing over her.

"The universe is changing," Kral said. "We will help shape it into a better place for all to live and thrive."

Becca smiled. She liked the sound of that.

Chapter Twenty

"Becca," Kral said. "We're here."

"Hmm, what?" She blinked, sitting up and glancing around blearily. "Where am I? Why is everything so shiny?"

Kral laughed. He kept his hand on her back, steadying her. Her fatigue was still obvious.

"We've reached Earth," Kral said. "We're right above your home."

Her home. Would she want to return to it?

Everything between them had happened so fast. Becca had been through so much. He didn't want to push more changes on her. At the same time, he couldn't bear the thought of being apart.

"Oh, wow," she said. "That was fast."

He smiled. "You slept most of the way."

"Is Sophie okay?" she asked. "And Amy?"

"They're both fine. It will still be some time before Amy is out of the healing chamber, but Nuar is happy with her progress." Kral stood next to Becca, his hands resting on her shoulders. "Sophie wishes to gather some of her belongings. After that, she says she wishes to stay on the

Arrow in one of our spare quarters."

"It makes sense that she'd feel safer here. I can't imagine what she must have gone through."

"We will protect her. And you." He hesitated for a few moments, then said, "I'm not sure how your customs work in this matter, but…will you stay here as well? With me?"

His hearts felt like they were frozen in place. He could barely breathe as he waited for her response.

She smiled gently, gazing at his chest, then lifted her hands and rested them above his hearts.

"That building beneath us isn't my home," she said. "My home is with you."

The pressure on his chest lifted. His hearts beat with renewed strength as he smiled down at her.

Becca pulled him down to her lips for a kiss. He grabbed her waist and crushed her against him, deepening the connection. When they were both breathless, he leaned back.

"May I take that as a yes?" he said, smirking.

"Yes," she said. Her smile faded. "We need to figure out what's going on with Sophie. Something is wrong, and she's not talking to me."

"She seems to be comfortable with Lar," Kral said. "He's our communications officer for a reason. If anyone can get to what's bothering her, it'll be him."

"I just wish she'd talk to *me*." Becca shook her head. "First Buddy, now Sophie. I'm used to being the one they come to."

"Much has changed. Give it time."

"I guess."

"Speaking of Buddy, however…" Kral rose from the bench and offered his hand. "I'm afraid my time is up when it comes to putting off his anger. He's waiting for us below."

"Really?" Becca's face lit up as she rose. "I can finally talk to him about everything. Come on."

Kral laughed at her renewed energy as she grabbed his hand and pulled him toward the main hatch. Lar and Sophie were already there, along with Dash.

The smile Sophie cast at them was strained. She inched closer to Lar as Becca and Kral joined them on the hatch. Oddly, Sophie was even eyeing Dash askance.

Becca was right. Something had definitely happened to her on the Tau Ceti base. Kral only hoped that Sophie would turn to her family for support when she was ready, and not isolate herself too much.

He looked up at Lar in time to see him staring at Sophie with a burning gaze. Unless Kral was mistaken, something was going on there as well. His hearts warmed at the thought that perhaps Sophie was Lar's soulmate. Kral couldn't think of a more perfect situation.

The hatch disconnected from the ship, then lowered into Becca and Sophie's back yard. The ship was fully cloaked this time. As more of the yard came into view,

Kral could see holo-emitters set up around the edges of the space. The entire property must be covered in a hologram.

Apparently, the Coalition wasn't taking any chances.

As the hatch lowered, Buddy and Nika came into view. Buddy was paler than usual and a muscle was twitching in his jaw. He sucked in a breath when his sisters came into view. Nika reached out and touched his arm. He squeezed her hand, then stepped forward and leapt up onto the hatch the moment it was low enough.

Buddy ran to Sophie and pulled her into a tight hug. He didn't seem to notice how she stiffened or the look of near panic in her eyes.

"I was so worried," he said. He pulled back so he could look her up and down. "Are you okay?"

Sophie pinched her lips together and nodded, but her eyes filled with tears. Buddy hugged her again, holding her for a long time while she clutched the back of his shirt. She was the one to finally pull away. Again, she stepped closer to Lar.

Buddy turned to Becca, shaking his head. There were deep lines etched between his brows.

"Come here," Buddy said, pulling her into a similar hug. Becca went to him gladly. Kral could feel the relief in her heart, spilling over into his.

He had a feeling his own relief would be short-lived.

After a much shorter time, Buddy released Becca and said, "What about Amy? I heard she was hurt."

"She's going to be fine," Becca said.

"*Going* to be?" Buddy shook his head. "With their technology, she should already be healed. How badly was she injured?"

"She's going to be fine." Becca kept her voice calm, but it didn't seem to be doing much.

Buddy turned to Kral.

"This is your fault," Buddy said. "I warned you to stay away. To leave them out of all this."

Before Kral could say anything, Becca shifted to stand in front of him.

"This is not his fault," Becca said. "It's the fault of the Tau Ceti who attacked them. They're the ones who pulled the trigger."

"They shot her?" Buddy actually took a step back. "The Tau Ceti?" He turned to Sophie. "Is that who had you?"

Sophie glanced away.

"Jesus." He ran his hands through his hair, then held them on top of his head for a moment. "Sophie, are you sure you're okay?"

This time, when he stepped toward her, she shook her head and jerked back.

Buddy let out a breath that seemed to empty him, disbelief and worry warring in his expression. He wheeled around toward Kral. "I told you to stay away."

"It wouldn't have made a difference." Sophie's voice

was small, a shadow of what she'd been like when Kral had met her only a day ago. Had it really been so recent?

"They already knew about you and the Cygnians," Sophie said. "They were already watching us."

Buddy looked stricken. Kral wanted to reach out to his friend, but knew it wouldn't be welcome yet. As with Sophie, this healing would take time.

Sophie opened her mouth as if she wished to say more, then snapped it shut. Steely resolve flowed into her expression. Kral thought she had never looked more like Becca than in that moment.

"Assigning blame isn't going to help us," Becca said. "And be glad I'm taking the high road, because I'm pissed as hell you kept this from us all."

"I was just trying to keep you all safe," Buddy said.

"I know." Becca stepped forward and hugged him. "Now that we know what's going on, we can take actual steps to protect ourselves."

Becca released Buddy and moved back to Kral's side. She interlaced their fingers, palms pressed together.

"I want training and information," she said. "For me and my sisters. Those Tau Ceti guys that came after us were only soldiers. I want to know who's giving the orders so we can take them down."

Buddy was staring at their clasped hands. He let out a huge breath.

"This can't work out," he said. "You and Kral. He's a

prince, for crying out loud. Did he not tell you that?"

"I did," Kral said. "And so did my parents."

Buddy's eyebrows rose. He turned his gaze back to Becca. "You talked to his parents?"

"She made quite an impression with them," Kral said.

"But what about the challenge?" Buddy asked. "I mean, there's no way she can—"

"You leave that to me." Becca glanced up at Kral and said, "I have some ideas there, but need a little time to work out the details."

Kral smiled as he gazed down at his soulmate. "I look forward to you revealing your strategy."

Her eyes smoldered as she leaned closer. "Oh, I'm not revealing anything. Not until I take you down."

Kral reached up and buried his fingers in her dark hair, tilting her head back so he could claim her lips in a branding kiss. Becca grabbed his shoulders, meeting his passion with her own fire.

Buddy let out a pained groan. "That's my sister, man. Come on."

Kral hadn't known he could laugh and kiss someone at the same time. But he and Becca both were smiling when they broke off the kiss. He kept her in his embrace, she with her arms tight around his waist.

"Get used to it," Kral said. "Because now that I have Becca in my arms, I'm never letting her go."

Becca laughed and gazed up at him with such love and

affection he thought his hearts might burst.

"Sounds good to me," she said.

Epilogue

Lar returned to his quarters, his thoughts weighing on him with the force of a gravity well. He could tell himself what he wished about hearing the sisters' voices—that he had only been moved by their harmony.

He could even explain away how his hearts altered their beat when he heard Sophie speak. But when he had touched Sophie, he had felt...something.

Something that he dared not name.

An incoming transmission drew his attention. He opened the channel and a hologram flickered into being. The image of Queen Ehmach stood in the room with him, as real as if she were there.

"Kral has lost his way," Ehmach said.

Lar shook his head. "I'm not sure. His bond with Becca seems real, as does Nuar's bond with Lian."

Her frown deepened. "It's a delusion. A dangerous delusion that will lead our people to ruin."

"What if it isn't?" Lar said. "What if our soulmates are here on Earth?"

"You swore an oath," Ehmach shouted.

"I know. But surely if I were to find—"

Ehmach spoke over him, her voice as sharp and cold as the crystal armor she wore. "You chose to make an oath to put my son above all others until the day you die. The word of a Cygnian is strong. But *that* oath among our house is sacred."

He shouldn't have dared to think she might release him from it. Only death could.

Bowing his head, he placed his fists next to his hearts.

"I understand," he said.

Ehmach stared at Lar in heavy silence. Then she said, "You will be tempted."

"I will endure it."

Ehmach said no more. She held him with her piercing stare for a while longer, her eyes blazing like citrine suns.

The hologram winked out.

Lar's hearts felt as if they were breaking. He believed their soulmates were here, on Earth. Ehmach had blinded herself to the truth. She was too focused on the outcome she expected, the path she had laid out for them all.

It didn't matter for Lar. He couldn't have a soulmate. Could never claim one. He had made the most sacred oath of his house. The most sacred oath of all Cygnians.

Kral had to come before all others until the day Lar died. If Lar bonded with a soulmate, he knew that she would take that place in his hearts.

She would become his everything.

He tried very hard not to think of Sophie.

And failed.

—

Thank you so much for reading *Kral: A Scifi Alien Warriors Romance*! I know some of you have been waiting for this one for a long time. I hope you loved it! Kral was done waiting, too. He'll have to wait a little longer to see what Becca has in store for her challenge (as well as the other Cygnian soulmates from Earth), but don't worry! She and I have plans...

The other warriors in Kral's prism have their hopes up, and each of them is searching for that special Earthling who will make their hearts beat in unity. An epic adventure awaits us all as they find their soulmates and make them their own. Keep reading for a sneak peek at the third *Cygnian 7* novel, *Lar: A Scifi Alien Warriors Romance!*

Lar: A Scifi Alien Warriors Romance

Cygnian 7
Book Three

Chapter One

Harbor, Kansas
Sol System - Planet 3
Earth:

Sophie jerked back as the blade hummed through the air, heading straight for her neck. She blocked it at the last moment. Her sword emitted a shower of sparks as it collided against the other energy weapon. The impact jolted Sophie all the way to her elbows, making her fingers tingle painfully. She shook her hand and gripped the hilt tighter as she staggered back a few paces.

Thank God I'm wearing the Cygnian wristbands, she thought as the tingling receded.

The wristbands were generating a reassuring pale golden light that coated her body, forming a protective shield. Sophie felt a surge of strength course through her muscles from the special augmentation she had activated. Otherwise, her weapon would have fizzled out under the impact.

Her adrenaline spiked as she twisted to keep her opponent in her line-of-sight. Her heart beat faster, echoing in her ears like the beat of a sound system with the bass turned up too high. As she waited for an opening, she wished she could say her adversary was doing the same, but all she *had* were openings.

She gulped in gasping breaths. Sweat dripped from her chestnut and sun-streaked hair under her collar and ran along her spine, making her skin prickle. She resisted the urge to squirm as it rolled below the waistband of the jeans she had borrowed from her sister, Becca. Every joint and muscle in her body ached.

I have to be better than this.

Light flashed over the milky-white crystal of the opalescent walls of the *Arrow's* training room, but she maintained her focus on the fight. Her sneakers squeaked on the polished crystal floor, making her wince. She ignored the dull ache in her rear-end that reminded her of the consequences of hitting the unpadded surface of the training room floor. Rolling her neck to ease the tension in her shoulders, she noticed how her opponent's eyes followed the movement.

Sophie decided to take advantage of his distraction and charged, lifting her weapon above her head. She brought her sword down with all her enhanced strength, even though she knew it would have little effect.

Her opponent parried her attack, easily knocking her blade away. Sophie spun around, hoping for an opening. Of course, her strategy didn't work. The clash between the two swords engaging created another shower of sparks that danced outward in a brilliant, blinding display of light. This time, her opponent didn't put any effort into pushing her away. They ended up nose-to-nose.

Her sun kissed nose to his very blue one.

Her deep brown eyes to his warm golden ones.

Her panting breath to his soft smile.

He is so gorgeous...

It was so easy to get distracted by Lar when he was near her—especially when they were sparring. She never felt more alive. Her skin tingled, her heart raced. Even when they weren't sparring, she felt like she couldn't quite catch her breath.

She only wished she could catch his attention. His cobalt-blue skin gleamed like the crystal walls around them. Her fingers twitched with the desire to touch him and explore the abundance of muscles that covered his body. His eyes were glowing like twin suns on a summer day, warming her soul as he returned her gaze. His hair fell down his back in dozens of indigo braids and a thick beard hid what she guessed was a jaw strong enough to match the rest of him. She wondered if he could sense her attraction or even shared it.

Stay focused. Think of Hayley.

Sophie repeated the chant. Hayley, her best friend in the universe, was out there somewhere, alone and at the mercy of the Tau Ceti—or worse. Unbidden memories pushed through the wall she had erected around them.

Tau Ceti Epsilon Base
Ceres Dwarf Planet
Sol Asteroid Belt
Two days earlier:

The taste of scorched popcorn and bile filled Sophie's mouth as she slowly woke up. Her back ached. She was lying on something cold and hard. What was she doing on a cold metal table? She had been about to start a sisters' movie night with her older sister, Becca, and her youngest sister, Amy. Becca was still out on her walk, but Amy...

Amy!

Pain pierced Sophie's brain right between her eyes as she jolted upright. She clenched her eyes shut, pressing her forehead with the heels of her palms, and tried not to throw up. As soon as the nausea began to pass, she looked at her surroundings. The room she was in was small, with grayish-brown metal walls. She was sitting on a bench that was attached to one of them. There was a toilet in one corner, along with a sink.

"Gross," Sophie murmured.

She stood slowly, gripping the bench as her legs wobbled beneath her. The room felt like it was spinning. She kept one hand on the wall as she tried to learn more about where she was and what had happened. The walls were completely smooth except for the outline of a door. There was a small rectangle etched in it at about eye level and a larger one at waist height.

Her stomach sank. She had seen doors like these in Amy's favorite crime shows. Prison doors.

Amy wasn't here. Something had happened to her. The memories trickled in as Sophie's head cleared.

Three men had broken into their house dressed in silver catsuits like something out of a 50's B sci-fi movie. Hayley's ex-boyfriend, Dean, had been with them, dressed considerably better, but he had morphed into some sort of shapeshifting monster. The men in silver had fired an alien-looking weapon. They had... They had shot Amy!

Sophie's stomach roiled and her heart sped up in her chest. Her skin prickled painfully. Amy was hurt, and Sophie had no idea where she was. She didn't know where she was herself. She had to escape and find her younger sister.

Sophie carefully studied the walls. There had to be an access panel or a control switch to open the door from inside. Her vision was still bleary from sleep and the drug they had used to knock her out. She rubbed her eyes to clear them and surveyed the room again.

On her third pass, she found a small rectangle etched into the metal near the door. Its outline was barely visible, but there was a spot that was scratched, as if someone had been trying to pry it open. Sophie ran her fingertip over the spot, feeling the roughness of the abraded metal. The edge was even raised a bit there. All she needed was something strong enough and flat to pry it open further.

She glanced down at her charm bracelet. They hadn't taken it, thank God. She didn't know what she'd do if she lost it. She hugged her wrist to her chest, thinking of Hayley. They always said their matching charm bracelets kept them connected, no matter what. Now it was going to help get Sophie out of this.

She unhooked a flat, solid charm and started picking at the spot where the panel was scratched. Her hands were shaking. She wiped her sweaty fingers on the back of her jeans and took a deep breath. Then another. When she felt calmer, she started working on the spot with her charm. She didn't know how much time she had before someone or something came through the door. It felt like it took forever, but eventually she wedged the charm into the tiny gap between the panel and the wall.

"Yes!"

Her heart raced faster as she managed to get her fingernails behind the panel and pry it a little farther out of place. Her nerves were so tight, she could barely breathe. Something jabbed against her fingers, and there was a flash of light on metal. Sophie yelped and flinched, dropping her charm. The panel snapped back into place with a tink.

"Dammit!"

She looked down at the offending item that had caused her to lose her progress and her brain just stopped. She couldn't understand what she was seeing. Her heart felt like it was lodged in her throat as she bent down and picked up the charms. Both of them.

The one she had been using to pry open the panel made sense. The other didn't. It was a half-heart charm with "Fs VAR" engraved on it. Sophie's hands were shaking as she brought up her bracelet and found the charm she had bought for herself and Hayley that year for their birthdays. Sophie held the half-heart charm she had found inside the panel against hers, where "BF 4-E" was engraved.

They matched up perfectly. Sophie had special-ordered them so that the charms would be an absolutely unique pair. This had to be Hayley's charm, but she had told Sophie that it was lost in the mail and she hadn't received it. That had been months ago.

Sophie staggered to the bench and sat down, her head spinning and tears burning in her eyes. She held up the charms side-by-side, trying to figure out what it all meant.

Only one thing made any sense at all. Hayley had been here. They had kept her prisoner.

The door swung open and Sophie quickly slid the

charm into her pocket. A man entered wearing yet another sci-fi costume, this one bronze with odd fins on the shoulders. He told her he was one of the three alien soldiers who had broken into their house. Tobek. He brought her food and water, and what she needed most of all—hope.

Hayley had made a deal with him to try to keep Sophie and her family safe from Dean. That's why Tobek had purposefully thrown off his fellow soldier's aim when the other man, Jaxa, had fired at them. Tobek didn't know why Dean was interested in Sophie's family, but now, he was her only hope of finding Hayley.

That was until the next time Sophie saw Tobek—being carried into her cell, held aloft by his throat in the grasp of an enormous man who turned out to be Kral, crown prince of the Cygnians.

Unless it was Dean in disguise. Unless it was another trick.

Kral was followed by Becca and two of Kral's warriors, Bron and Lar. Sophie didn't believe it was a genuine rescue until she saw Lar.

Instinctively she sensed she could trust him with her life, her heart, her everything. It was as though she had known him forever. She could feel him, knew that he was telling her the truth. He was the only person she could trust.

"Sophie? Are you ready to continue?"

Lar's gentle voice snapped Sophie back to the training room. A continuous pulse of energy raced up and down her spine. It spread out to her limbs, making her fingers tingle almost painfully. Lar's gaze was so bright, her eyes burned. How long had they been staring at each other? She lifted a hand and rubbed her temple, trying to get her bearings.

Breathe, Sophie. I'm on the Arrow. *Deep breath. I'm with Lar. Breathe. I'm safe. Just breathe.*

She felt calmer. While *she* was on the *Arrow*, Hayley was not. Sophie had to find her friend. There was no one else who even knew Hayley was missing. She couldn't afford the luxury of a nervous breakdown until Hayley was safe.

Hayley needs me to stay focused. After she's home, then I can have a total meltdown. Right now, I need to learn everything I can to get her back.

If Sophie answered Lar with words, they would start talking and she might let something slip. No one could know about Hayley. Not when there was a shapeshifting alien mercenary targeting Sophie's family who could take anyone's form.

Just the thought of Dean finding out that Sophie was on to him was enough to make her stomach sour. If he found out she knew about him, she would lose the only advantage she had. She would lose her only chance to find out what he had done with Hayley.

"Sophie?" Lar prompted again, his voice even softer, her name like a caress.

The only time he let them be close was when they were sparring like this. Sophie wasn't ready for that closeness to be over. The prospect sent her spiraling back toward the panic she had just clawed her way out of. She answered by lashing out with the leg closest to him, wrapping her knee around his in a move that should have knocked him off balance and thrown him to the floor.

It didn't work. It did, however, send frissons of pleasure racing up and down her spine. Her skin rose in tingling goosebumps, her heart beat faster, and her mouth went dry. Heat pooled low in her belly. He was still standing so close.

Lar cast a strained smile at her and her stomach did a flip. His eyes glowed brighter and she felt some kind of rumbling vibration emanating from him. It permeated through her muscles, relaxing and arousing her at the same time. She leaned closer, their blades touched again, emitting a crackling sound.

"That might work on a human, but not on me," he said.

He pushed against her sword. With her leg still half-wrapped around his, she lost her balance and fell backwards, landing hard on the crystal floor. Pain lanced through her body as old bruises were joined by new ones.

Lar stood above her, still smiling that gentle smile of his. "You need to remember that your opponents will not always be human. Find their weaknesses. Exploit them."

"That doesn't sound very Cygnian," Sophie said.

He shrugged. "You're from Earth. We need to work with what you have."

He extended his hand toward her. They had never touched—not like this. Her heart leapt frantically in her chest as she reached for him. She was about to take his hand when his eyes widened and he suddenly stepped back, his gait stiff. He winced as if he was in pain.

What had just happened? Sophie scrambled to her feet, humming the control note for the wristbands that would deactivate all of their current functions. Her sword vanished with a fizzling sound.

"Are you okay?" she asked.

"I'm fine." He smiled at her, but she could see the lines of strain around his eyes.

Something was wrong. Something he wasn't telling her about. She reached out to him again. "Are you sure?"

Before her hand could connect, he turned away, moving out of reach. He deactivated his energy blade, his back toward her.

"You're very good with a sword," Lar said.

Was he trying to break the tension of that strange exchange with humor? It didn't seem like him. Cygnians might not even have a similar idiom in their culture. Sophie decided to let it pass.

"I dated a guy in college who was super into fencing," she said. "I really liked it, so I kept training after we broke up."

A stronger wave of vibration hit her. She gasped as it delved through her muscles to ring in her bones. The shivers down her back turned to prickles, like all the hair on her spine was standing on end. She rubbed her arms to make the fresh—and less than pleasant—goosebumps go away.

"Thanks for helping me learn how to use these Cygnian wristbands," she said, trying to distract herself as much as anything else while the vibration subsided.

"You're pushing yourself very hard," Lar said. "Not even Becca is training as much as you are or studying our ways with such intensity. It makes me wonder... Why are you?"

Sophie shrugged. "Well, Becca and Kral have other things to do, if you know what I mean."

Oh, damn. Did I say that out loud?

Lar arched a dark blue eyebrow. "I suppose you have a point."

She pinched her lips together to keep from embarrassing herself further with a quip about Becca having access to two "points" thanks to Cygnian anatomy. Apparently, Cygnians were fairly similar to human men, only times two. Sophie felt her cheeks heat, knowing they must be beet red. She hoped Lar would assume it was from their sparring and not the erotic thoughts she couldn't get out of her head.

Oh, but that is a nice setup, she couldn't help wickedly thinking.

"You still haven't answered my question," Lar said.

How could Sophie get out of this? She looked away, trying to think of what to say while her mind spun. She wished she could tell him the truth.

Because my best friend is out there somewhere, being held captive either by the sadistic scientist who ran the secret Tau Ceti base in our solar system or a Scorpiian mercenary. Rescuing her is my highest priority even though I know there's a war going on and everyone is needed elsewhere. I just have to keep trying to find her no matter what and do whatever it takes to bring her safely home.

Her heart sank as she thought of what would happen next. If Sophie told Lar the truth, he would tell Kral. Then Kral would tell Becca and who knew how many others. The more people who knew, the better the chances were that Dean would find out. Heck, one of the people they told could actually *be* Dean. He had tricked Sophie into thinking he was Hayley for months. Sophie couldn't even trust her dog anymore.

Her eyes filled with tears at the thought. She missed

spending time with Dash so much, and knew Dash must feel the same. If it really was her dog, she hated the thought of how it must be confusing and hurtful to Dash that Sophie was keeping her distance. They hadn't done her agility practice or anything.

Sophie hadn't been able to even be near Dash. Instead, she was relying on Nuar's Earthling soulmate, Lian, for help. Thank goodness Lian had her Saint Bernard, Ed, for Dash to hang out with and knew how to care for a dog. Sophie would be relying on Lian to care for Dash during the next part of her personal mission.

She sniffed and blinked to clear her eyes. "Listen, I actually... I need to talk to Rom. Is he around?"

She gasped as a wave of hurt and betrayal rippled through her. Where had that come from? She didn't understand why she would feel that way. She must be more messed up from her ordeal than she realized.

For a second, she swore she saw Lar's lip curl up in a sneer. Did he not like Rom? They were in the same prism. She was still learning about their group, but she thought that meant they were all connected somehow, on a deep soul level. She supposed they didn't necessarily have to like each other, but Lian had described it as "kind of an epic bromance between seven Cygnian dudes."

"I would take care when dealing with Rom if I were you," Lar said, his words coming out a bit stiff. "He is... I believe the Earth word of your region is 'a player.'"

Sophie laughed. She could totally see that, with Rom's smoldering violet eyes and soulful smile. But Lar was the only Cygnian who held her interest. He was the one who made her heart beat faster just by walking into the room, the one who made her feel better, even when it seemed like everything was hopeless.

"I'm not in any danger there," Sophie said. "I just... I was just going to ask for his help with something." As soon as she figured out how to ask without giving away her secrets.

Rom was the Cygnians' pilot, and Sophie needed to get back to the Tau Ceti base on Ceres. Back to where she had been held prisoner by Dean and his minions. Back to where they'd held Hayley.

"Perhaps I can assist you instead," Lar suggested. Again, his eyes widened, as if he had surprised himself with his offer. His jaw snapped shut with a clack.

If he could be the one to take Sophie back to Ceres, that would be perfect. She felt safer with him than with anyone she had ever met. If they were alone together, she might even be able to tell him about Hayley, if she swore him to secrecy first. He seemed like the kind of person who kept his word. Sophie liked that about him. If she was honest with herself—and she usually was—she liked everything about him.

If only he felt the same way about me.

—

Sophie and Lar are in for quite the roller coaster ride. Seriously, I'm afraid my muse is going to put them through the wringer. Still, I can't wait to share their story with you! And the rest of the Cygnian warriors can't wait to meet their soulmates. This series is so much fun to write! The adventure will pick up right where we left off in *Lar: A Scifi Alien Warriors Romance*.

If you want to learn more about Kral and the other Cygnian warriors' universe, you can check out *The Department of Homeworld Security* adventures. Many of the novellas have been collected in the first two series omnibuses, *The Department of Homeworld Security Omnibus 1* and *The Department of Homeworld Security Omnibus 2*. Or you can pick and choose with the individual novellas.

I'd love to keep in touch. Join my newsletter at sendfox.com/cassandrachandler to hear about all the adventures happening in Cassland. And if you enjoyed this book, please consider leaving a review at your favorite book review site. I'd really appreciate it—reviews help readers and authors alike!

Thank you for reading *Kral: A Scifi Alien Warriors*

Romance!

Cassandra Chandler

About the Author

USA Today Bestselling author Cassandra Chandler uses her vivid imagination to make the world more interesting, spawning the ideas she turns into her enthralling Science Fiction Romances and darkly evocative Paranormal and Urban Fantasy Romances. Fast-paced and funny, lighthearted or dark, her stories will introduce you to characters you'll fall in love with and worlds you long to explore.